GW00761063

MISDIRECTION

MARTIN LINK

To Ann and Todd for their endless patience and support.

There are many others I will not list in case I miss someone, but you know who you are—thank you.

CONTENTS

ONE

T his dark and menacing evening, the cycle ride to my office has proved to be more challenging than normal with a brutal tailwind turning my fluorescent orange high-vis into a sailcloth and the slush from the sleeting rain making the road treacherous. By the time I slide to a halt at the complex, even with my industrial waterproofs, I am soaked to the skin and my hands and face are numb.

The entrance is austere, with plain, green-plastic-coated chain-link fencing disguising its high-tensile steel core. The only giveaway that this is a highly secure site is the small green box next to the gate latch, which has the obligatory tiny, red, flashing lamp. The equally bland olive-green sign next to the gate states simply: Authorised Persons Only Beyond This Point. However, the characters GCHQ (Government Communications Headquarters) at the bottom-right corner add gravitas and hint at this being the most secure complex in Cheltenham—indeed, in the whole country. It is warning enough to most visitors without advertising the omnipresent building and boundary-mounted CCTV, thermal scanners, facial recognition, and other surveillance technology that currently verify me.

After only fifteen seconds, I am cleared, and the little lamp on the post now shines green. The bombproof latch smoothly and silently releases. The gate sits ajar as if daring me to enter. The firm and efficient voice of a security guard clearly advises my next steps. "Good evening, Mr Norton. Please proceed to the cycle rack and secure your bicycle. Then report to reception." I push my cycle through the gate, which I close behind me, and the latch gives a purposeful clunk as it locks. The system knows my route, and if I deviate, the picture from the camera tracking me will be placed on the screen in front of the security guard.

At reception my iris is scanned, my hard-copy credentials checked, and Tony, whom I am meeting, is informed of my arrival. Whilst waiting, I take this opportunity to go to the adjacent wet room and disrobe.

Tony meets me on the company side of the turnstile. He is over six feet tall, with cheeky eyes and baby curls. He has an easy charm, which makes him very popular with the opposite sex. He is also twenty years younger than me and relishes the fact. "Hi, Lucas, you old fart. Lovely to see you. How is the incontinence and memory loss these days? Still hiding your own Easter eggs?"

"Lovely to see you, too. You're starting to look quite grown up, apart from the blond kiss-curls. Have you started to shave yet?"

"I'm light brown, not blond, you idiot!"

"On the inside, I meant." I ignore his outstretched arm and give him a bear hug, which makes him recoil. He isn't at all tactile, but having known me for twelve years, he accepts that I am—and that if he avoids my hug, it will last a lot longer. I must admit, I do get a kick out of seeing him squirm. "Smile, Tony, we're on TV!" I say, clutching him even tighter.

"Sod off. The guards will take the piss for weeks." Laughing, we head to the lifts, my shoes squelching across the marble.

As we walk along the fourth-floor corridor to his office, the external security lights showcase the sleeting rain hammering horizontally onto the windows of this shiny, new, conspicuous, green-glass building. The "doughnut," as it is nicknamed, is a far cry from the old Nissen huts which it replaced in 2003. Ten days until Christmas, and I, for one, hope this miserable sleet will turn to snow.

Tony's office has glass walls and grey furniture matching the grey carpet and grey filing cabinets. The team desks are in the usual open-plan arrangement, but in neat, four-person carrels with grey, shoulder-height partitions. It's an in-joke that everything in the building has to be battleship grey.

One consolation is the efficient air conditioning, with its humidity control and CO_2 monitoring; these are essential, as there are no opening windows. Despite it giving me a slight feeling of claustrophobia, the ultra-high level of security makes me feel safe; it is like being back in the womb. And it's so, so quiet.

Tony glances at the array of computer screens on his desk to check the electronic charges as they monitor chit-chat on the airwaves across the world. It's another in-joke that if a fly farts in Finland, this place will hear it, determine its speed, direction, and altitude—all before the fly says, "Beg pardon."

Peering over Tony's shoulder, I ask, "Is it pretty quiet here at the moment?"

"Mostly. Always something going off somewhere, but nothing that's a panic."

"Is the lovely Coops still working here?"

"Oh, yes. In fact, Coops is on duty tonight. I expect you'll get your usual welcome, but I've not told her you're coming." Coops—Katy Cooper—is a petite, twenty-four-year-old, pretty brunette with a level head that belies her youth. Her sense of humour is legendary, as are her computer skills. Also unusual for her tender years, she absolutely loves John Wayne—something we have in common and often joke about.

"Brilliant. I've not seen her for ages. What's she doing here now? I hear a lot of changes are being made."

"Oh, yeah, Coops is now senior engineer on our electronic monitoring setup. As for me, I still look after the communications side of the team. It's just the two of us tonight, and we are covering this entire floor."

"Blimey. I did hear they were cutting back. Or are the systems doing even more of the work?"

"It's almost completely automatic now. We just babysit the stuff really, attending to it when it has a tantrum or needs its ink cartridges changed. We are on until six in the morning, when the next pair of childminders take over."

"European shift pattern—that *is* new. So, any chance of a coffee? This seems to be a dry old place."

"You drink too much blooming coffee."

"Whatever."

"Well, you'll be pleased to know that we have a bean-to-cup coffee machine and free-vend Red Bull, though my request for a pool table and leather sofa was rebuffed. Come on, I'll introduce you to my own blend of beans!"

Just as Tony and I reach the door to the corridor, Coops

bursts in. "Hey, Tony," she exclaims excitedly, "the monitoring programme has identified an email with the words *bomb*, *security*, *terror,* and *cash*—that's a full house, and no mistake."

The communications traffic of the world is monitored 24/7. Among the graded register of thirty or so high-level words are the four she's just found. They are grouped very near the top of the list, and when found together in a single email, they attract the full attention of the authorities.

"Wow, those are top keywords," Tony replies eagerly. "They couldn't get us to look at them more closely if they tried." And in his John Wayne drawl, he added, "Go geddum, liddle lady."

I step out from behind Tony, and with open arms, I beam at Coops. "Mr Norton!" she squeals like a lost offspring. "Fabulous to see you; this is brill." We hug, and as always, she attempts to squeeze every last bit of air out of me. But this time, I'm released quickly—the email message is her first priority. "I'm sorry, but no time to chat now. You must both come and look at this message! It's the highest-level alarm we've had in years."

Coops's little haven is in the adjoining room. Her desk is really two butted together, and the grey, shoulder-height partitions are peppered with memorabilia. There are Kinder egg toys, unfathomable puzzles, holiday photos, unbreakable cyphers, and graphic scribblings. It resembles a kleptomaniac's nest—but move something at your peril, as Coops knows where everything is to the millimetre: the ultimate proof of chaos theory.

The three of us huddle in front of massive computer screens while Coops clatters around her keyboard with blisteringly quick, two-finger typing. She flips from one monitor to the other, absorbing information before I've even registered that the screen image has changed. Almost immediately, she finds there are now two emails from the same source, transmitted within three minutes of each other.

Something is obviously not right, especially as this is the first time I have seen four words at this level used in a single email, let alone two in quick succession. But then we discover that the first email had bounced back to the sender's smartphone: invalid email address. *Idiot!* The second email is delivered successfully and instantly gets a reply: simply, " 2 "

Coops runs tracing software to find the owners of these email addresses. They appear to be inaugural emails from new accounts originating from a private school in London now closed for the Christmas holidays.

Straight away, Coops attempts to break into that school's computer system to try to establish the hacker's location. This can take some time for the average techie, but Coops's best is twenty-three minutes into the FBI mainframe. School systems are generally not overly secure, and sure enough, after a couple of minutes, Coops is in. But she swears softly. "Sod it. I'm going to leave a tracer program on the school's system in case they come back, and also run an international trace for earlier comms. These guys are bloody good; I've no clue as to where this hack originated."

Coops and Tony now run tracking and tracing programs across billions of world-wide communications. Using similar algorithms, our FBI colleagues in Virginia are no doubt analysing the self-same messages hoping they can advise us with the answer.

I am not much help these days and decide to get the coffees. "Coops, I guess you still take yours with three sugars?"

No response; she's totally focused on the job in hand.

I repeat myself. "Guys, coffee?"

"Oh, yeah," Coops answers, "three sugars and a Mars bar— my soul needs chocolate, my head needs sugar!"

When I get back, Tony has already initiated the next stage by running a full international mobile comms check against that smartphone covering the past seven days. After a few minutes, he finds a call from three days ago emanating from central Rome, with its destination somewhere near Berkeley Square, London. Despite a massive amount of interference, words detected are *Dover*, *Lewes*, *Newcastle*, and mention of *fifty-eight minutes*. The call does give a good voice signature, so now we can monitor comms traffic for that specific person.

One minute later, and from the same mobile in Rome, there

is a short text to the London phone:
11210211640553757107345.

One of Coops's monitors is flashing a message that the mobiles are now dead and the email accounts closed. Her plan to leave tracking software on the school's systems would come to naught. She frowns. "Not a hint of them being there; they've gone without a smidgen of a trail. They really are bloomin' good. Is this the FBI up to its tricks just to pee me off?"

Tony shakes his head and, without turning from his screen, mutters, "It's bloody annoying. We've done well considering, but there's a fair bit more work to join the dots."

"I'll track these swine down," Coops pronounces vehemently, "no matter how much coffee and chocolate it takes!"

To make myself useful, I complete a summary report of tonight's events and email it to Jeff, head of antiterrorism, Military Intelligence Section 5—MI5—London, along with Coops's and Tony's detailed analysis. I know my report will go straight through to Jeff's Blackberry, and so I wait for the return call on my mobile. Sure enough, a few minutes later, Jeff's name comes up on my phone. "Hi, Jeff, got the report then?"

"Yes, thanks for that. Any initial thoughts on those towns? Or that twenty-four-digit number?"

"Dunno about the towns, we are trying to get more intel to correlate the geography. And that number is a real sod; it's definitely making my gut uncomfortable."

"Well, let me know immediately you get any developments, but in any case, I will see you in London the day after tomorrow for your interview."

"Right! Can't wait, though I'm a bit nervous."

"No need. I'm sure it's a formality, really."

"Thanks for the reassurance."

"Oh, and by the way, Lucas, for your ears only—I've moved us to threat level critical. Not seen that since 7/7."

TWO

I walk along Albert Embankment, enjoying the predawn morning breeze and the slapping of the Thames' high tide onto the riverbanks' wall below me. The old, black, cast-iron street lamps shed light pools across the smooth-worn, cobbled walkway. The dappled light and smell of a nearby coal fire recall memories of old black-and-white movies of Thames barges and wind-powered cutters. I imagine top-hatted villains skulking in smog-filled alleyways, their grotesque faces glimpsed in soft shadows from the illumination of gas lamps as they await their cohort of cutlass-armed smugglers to unload contraband of oilskin-bagged tea and kegs of brandy on to the mud banks of the river.

I am brought back to reality when I see the first CCTV tentacle of the pale sandstone walls of MI5's head office, Thames House. These tentacles become ever more pervasive the closer I get, and as I walk through the gated entrance, I almost believe I can see a camera lens blink. Although I've been inside dozens of times, reception still makes me apprehensive. One of the heavily armed guards confronts me. "Good morning. Please may I see evidence of your appointment and contact?"

I hand over Jeff's headed letter. The guard makes a brief phone call for verification before allowing me through to the hallowed company side of the turnstiles. I am discreetly checked over for anything remotely dangerous. The humourless guard advises, "Mr Goddin will be with you in a few minutes."

I make myself comfortable on a sumptuous, brown leather sofa next to the table covered with copies of *Security Magazine*, the *Times,* and the *Guardian*.

I've barely time to browse the latest issue of *InfoSecurity* magazine before Jeff appears. He hasn't changed a bit. Well over six feet tall, he is still bright-eyed and, as usual, impeccably dressed—like a Moss Bros mannequin. The only difference, since I last saw him, is that his hairline has receded a little further, giving rise to the beginnings of a widow's peak.

We shake hands enthusiastically and start chatting as we take a lift to the twelfth floor. "So, Jeff, it's been a while. How the hell are you? And Kate and the kids?"

"Kate's fine; she's still running the doctor's surgery, and the kids are doing their mocks for their GCSEs."

"But...how about you?" I press further. "Are you still burning the candle at both ends?"

"Flipping busy at the moment. I'm hot-desking with MI6 on a special international antiterrorism task force. How's your brood?"

"Helen's now assistant head at Saint Andrew's private school in Eastbourne, Molly has just started her GCSEs, and Daisy her A levels."

"Blimey, they do grow up quick. And how was the journey up from the Sunshine Coast?"

"Not bad, no delays. Just the usual jostling at Clapham Junction."

Jeff's office is in the corner of a large, open-plan room on the twelfth floor. It has a breathtaking view eastward across the Thames to the Houses of Parliament, whilst to the west is the green-and-sandstone edifice that is MI6's head office, Vauxhall Cross—or the "Greenhouse," as it's nicknamed. The carpet and walls are in the same shades of grey as GCHQ with near-identical levels of blandness, and the starkness is exacerbated by the green-tinted, opaque glass partition walls, frosted to about waist height. The desktops, pedestal drawers, and filing cabinets are also frosted green glass, with the main room in pods for specific teams. It's all so clean and sterile; it could double as an operating theatre.

As we walk into Jeff's office, the glass walls instantly become white and totally opaque— electric privacy glass - neat! Also, Jeff's desktop, unlike all the others we've passed, is black glass. I've only just registered this fact when it erupts into colour, revealing itself as a computer monitor, whilst simultaneously, a mirror on the glass wall transforms itself into a screen, startling me. A lifelike woman's face appears on the wall monitor and pronounces, "Good afternoon, Jeff. I see you have a guest." She

8

glances down at an invisible desk in front of her, apparently checking something, and continues, "Ah, yes. Good afternoon, Mr Norton. Would you like some refreshment?"

I gape at Jeff and walk up to the image on the screen. As I approach, she leans towards me and smiles. I swing round. "My God, Jeff! Things have certainly changed since my time here."

He chuckles. "You bet. So, go on, tell her what you want."

"What, speak to her?"

"Or you can say it to me."

I choose to look at Jeff as I order. "I'd like an Earl Grey tea please, with one sugar, a little milk, and maybe some biscuits."

"Excuse me, I'm over here!"

I turn. The tilted face is smiling at me quizzically. I clear my throat. "Uh…I'd like an Earl Grey tea with milk and one sugar please, and maybe a biscuit?"

"Thank you, Mr Norton, that will be a pleasure." The voice has a luxuriant, sexy tone with rolled Rs. The image slowly fades, and the screen goes blank.

I gape again at Jeff. "Bloody hell! Face recognition as well—that's amazing."

Jeff laughs. "Do you recognise her?"

"There is something vaguely familiar about her face, and the voice…" I frown, searching my memory.

"Go on, have a guess," he teases me.

"Is it someone famous?"

"I'll give you a clue: 'carry on.'"

"Just tell me. I'll be guessing all morning."

"OK, it's from *Carry On Screaming*."

"Well, blow me—of course! She's Fenella Fielding. Inspired. But how the hell did you replicate her?"

"Easy. Just got one of the techies to analyse her features and voice pattern from the film and build a self-learning algorithm. We've given her a twenty-thousand-word vocabulary."

"Incredible," I tell him. "The visual likeness is truly awesome."

"Yep. I just hope Fenella doesn't want royalties!"

Within five minutes, my tea is brought by the office junior

who says he's sorry, but there are only ginger nut biscuits and hopes they will suffice. I'm now convinced I could work here, and the "interview" with Jeff appears to progress well as we deal with the somewhat informal topics of family, hobbies, gadgets, and so on.

Then his phone rings. He peers at the screen to identify the caller, raises a finger briefly to indicate to me he will only be a minute, and takes the call. "Hi, Suzi, what's up? Oh, I see. Well, the new guy is right here. I'll check, but my money is on tomorrow." Jeff glances at me and grins. "OK, Suzi. I will let you know soonest, bye." He replaces the phone, leans back in his big, black, leather chair, and takes a long gulp of his coffee before casually asking, "When could you start?"

Knowing Jeff, I'm aware that he always has a card up his sleeve, and so this is probably a loaded question. "Contractually, one month's notice."

"Well, I cleared it with your boss, and you *can* start tomorrow. Only caveat is, he insists you take the odd call relating to existing cases."

I pretend to consider the offer for a moment before I nod. "That's fine by me," I say casually.

"Excellent. Oh, by the way, Suzi will be leading your team at Thames House. There's been a development on that data you sent from GCHQ. You can continue joining the dots on those towns, and the meaning of that damn number."

THREE

Dawn is almost breaking as I let my diesel Astra freewheel down the gently sloping road in neutral, so as not to wake the neighbours in this sleepy little private estate. I pass the small, tree-lined green, the Greensward, which in spring is picturesque with candy-blossom cherry trees and engraved benches donated by past residents' families. But on a bleak, wintry morning such as this, with the sea mist billowing around the trees and oak seats, it is cold and murky, and when my headlamps expose the fiery eyes of a fox, just a little spooky.

Once on the main highway, I accelerate up the steep hill exiting Friston and feel my ears pop as the chalky South Downs rise five hundred feet above sea level. As I approach the brow, the sea mist recedes, and as I round the bends, my headlamps reveal fields populated by ghost-white sheep and the occasional leafless wind-bowed tree. The temporary snow fencing reminds me of nature's ability to annually isolate our small village.

As always, at the summit of the steep, winding descent into Eastbourne, I am enchanted by the magnificent, speckled lights of the street lamps and the orange blush that stretches along the seafront from Beachy Head to Pevensey Bay. By the time I reach the town's centre, there is already a stir of activity.

I love this place and its air of gentility, especially in the early morning, with its cafés and shops quietly preparing for the leisurely morning rush of locals going to work. There are well-heeled elderly folk emerging for their cafetière before their daily perusal of the shops, and students larking about on the pavements, delaying arriving for the start of their lessons in the schools and colleges.

And of course, there are also the commuters, like me, heading to the train station to be shunted off to their work in mid-Sussex or London. One advantage of commuting from Eastbourne is that being a terminal station, you always get a comfortable seat; a second advantage is that it is blessed with new rolling stock. The journey to London may be thirty minutes longer than the more

11

popular Brighton run, but it's worth it to be able to snooze in relative comfort most of the way.

A further advantage is that there are still some free car parking streets as the council have not yet introduced town-wide metering. I always choose to park in Hartfield Square, just off The Avenue, as it is only a short walk from there to the station.

The square has a tranquil air, with its many specimen trees and perennials and the soothing splash from the small fountain at its centre. The surrounding bright-white, four-storey Victorian town houses conjure up for me a bygone era of horse-drawn carriages parked under gas street lamps, with snorted horse breaths swirling in the chill air, as they and their coachmen wait patiently for suited gentlemen and ladies in long, flowing dresses to emerge from black-gloss front doors.

By the time I enter the marbled floor of the station concourse, I am more than ready to be enticed by the aroma of fresh-roast coffee from the black-and-gold liveried mobile café. I buy a frothing latte, warm *pain au chocolat*, and then nip into WH Smith to get a *Times* newspaper before finding my platform and a quiet seat away from the entrance doors on the waiting train. I complete the crossword, finish my coffee, and snuggle into my duffel coat for a doze.

**

I wake up just before the train pulls into Clapham Junction and brace myself for the bustle of belligerent commuters at London's busiest rail station. The stampeding crowds on the platform are a shock to the senses after the unhurried politeness of fellow passengers boarding at Eastbourne. Fortunately, I only have to endure a short hop from here to Vauxhall Station, cross over Vauxhall Bridge, and then I have a brisk, five-minute walk to Thames House.

My greeting at the fortified reception desk of MI5 is less intimidating than twenty-four hours ago for my interview with Jeff. This is because I am now part of "the company", which is reflected in the warm welcome from the bespectacled and smartly dressed woman in the Human Resources department. She provides me with an outline of the day's induction, and then I am taken to the security orientation which includes the usual scanning and facial recognition. Additionally, I am subjected to iMoCap movement tracking and a chip implant; these procedures are new to me.

James, the young guy setting up the iMoCap gizmo, is definitely IT. His faded designer T-shirt, frayed jeans, and Nikes no doubt cost more than my M&S suit. He takes no notice of me until I express my curiosity about the gizmo, and then suddenly his eyes light up. "It's brill. Only had it a few months."

"So, what does it do, exactly?"

"Well, first off, it builds a simple model of you with your facial recognition as its reference point—a bit like an LS Lowry stick man really, but with your face on it. Then it scans and stores hundreds of thousands of reference points as I get you to move your arms, legs, and head, and then walk and run in front of its sensors."

"What, all in that little webcam thingy?"

"Yep. Cool, huh? This baby's sensors respond in thirteen billionths of a second."

"Bloody incredible. But what the hell's it for?"

"That's the really clever bit. Even ignoring the facial recognition, it's got a greater than ninety-five per cent chance of recognising you from your posture, gait, and all that, even if you're in silhouette!"

"Wow! I'm seriously impressed."

"OK. So let's get on with it." The next ten minutes is like a one-man hokey-cokey. Afterwards, he lets me see a replay, and it crosses my mind that not much would be required to turn my iMoCap into a gaming character—hopefully like one of those invincible guys in *Call of Duty*.

I am now, at last, able to sit and relax, watching James prepare the chip implant. I'm imagining this is like the Pet-ID chip implanted in a dog's neck, where you run a scanner over and it comes up with the owner's address. But when I mention this to James, he gives me a disparaging look and holds up the minute device in his palm. "No way, man! This equipment is *massively* advanced—latest on the planet."

"So what's it do, then?"

"Do you have a satnav in your car?"

"Yeah, it's cutting edge, with street-level pictures, too!"

"Well, this does all that, plus records your travel like a black box, and—get this, it also monitors your heart rate, biomagnetism, and brain activity."

"Bloody hell. So where is it implanted?"

"In the back of your neck, just above the hairline."

"Can I hold it and have a look close up?"

"No way: it has to be sterile. But I'll show you one I dropped on the carpet." He hands me something the size of a grain of rice, but unlike rice, it has a glinting, crystal quality, displaying a moving rainbow of colours, like spilt petrol in sunlight.

"That's it? No battery or wires?"

"That's it. And the next generation is even smaller, and with dozens more functions!"

I would like to keep the tiny crystal to show Helen, but I know that is out of the question. James grabs the chip back when he spots the uniformed nurse approaching. She is a rotund woman in her early fifties, with dark hair in a pudding-basin style. She displays a no-nonsense demeanour, and is obviously in a hurry. "Mr Norton?"

I'm distracted by the sheer size of her butcher's hands. "Yes."

"Please sit, and push down your shirt collar."

She holds a skin-sterilising swab in one hand, whilst in the other brandishing an unfeasibly large syringe with a needle reminiscent of a football pump adaptor. I tense up, fearing the worst. But I barely feel a thing as she tags me.

She then orders me to sit for five minutes in case I feel dizzy or nauseous, after which she escorts me to the canteen, where I grab a coffee. Fifteen minutes later, a young, crop-haired, dark-suited chap finds me and escorts me to my two-hour security briefing where I sign the Official Secrets Act—*again*. This is the third time in as many years, although each time, I've been told it's for perpetuity.

By then it is lunchtime, and I meet up with Jeff in the canteen. "So, Lucas, how did the morning go—all orifices present and correct?"

"Yeah, right. Very bloody funny. I was prepared for some advances, but not the chip implant, and the iMoCap reminds me of the Microsoft Kinect."

He gives me a wry smile. "Actually, as usual, that kit originates from UK agency research projects, where we've shared knowhow with the FBI—cloned in America. But having learnt from past experience, we held back a superior version of the technology, and with our lab's latest software, we have *enhanced* iMoCap."

I raise my eyebrows and say with derision, "Typical, Britain's brilliant at producing boffins, but not exploiting the associated business opportunities."

Knowing Jeff's eating habits, I'm not surprised he's brought a home-prepared tuna and mayo sandwich for his lunch. He is a health fanatic. But I choose a steak and kidney pudding from the canteen. Our choice of desserts follow a similar pattern; Jeff's is a Weight Watcher's banoffee, and mine, jam roly-poly and custard!

As I'm enjoying my pudding, I recall an image from my childhood: my dad, mum, and I are sitting at the dining table, when he jokes that he "likes Raquel Welch custard." When I enquired why, he said it had very large lumps, and that's when Mum light-heartedly clipped his ear and told him not to be lewd at the dinner table.

When I asked Mum what *lewd* meant, I got a clip round the ear as well, and told to eat my custard. I remember thinking at the time its lumps were in fact quite small. It was some years later, when sitting next to my dad watching the film *One Million Years BC*, that during Raquel's first scene he leant over to me and whispered, "Lumps." Immediately I knew what he meant.

Jeff waits politely for me to finish my cholesterol-boosting pudding. We then get two takeaway lattes from the canteen counter. We pause in the corridor before going our separate ways, and Jeff smiles. "Guess you're off to the armoury now, and then interrogation—sorry, interview methodology."

"Yep, off to the guns 'n' hoses induction. What about you?"

"I've got to get back to the office. There have been more rumblings about those communications you tracked down at GCHQ."

"So, what's the latest?"

"It's a long story. I'll brief you end of play, but if not, we'll probably touch base tomorrow." I watch him stride off down the corridor, initiating a call on his mobile as he goes. Then I make my way four levels below ground to the armoury.

I am met by what appears to be a retired Special Air Service officer in all-black fatigues and impossibly shiny black toecap boots. "Afternoon, Mr Norton," he says brusquely. "I'm Sergeant Hopkins—call me Sarge."

"Hello, Sarge," I reply as instructed.

He marches me through bombproof doors and along sharply lit, white-walled rooms to the presentation theatre. My eyes are popping with schoolboy amazement at the rack-upon-rack quantity of weaponry and tech.

After subjecting me to a short health and safety risk assessment video, Sarge hands me a brand new Glock 19, and we move down to a lower floor that houses the indoor range for a quick "evaluation." After half an hour of me shooting paper targets with every weapon imaginable, Sarge is satisfied. I sign for a normal-looking black leather briefcase full of gizmos including the Glock, bulletproof vest, iPhone, and a key ring micro-can of tracking spray. Techiest of all though, are the night-sight contact lenses including rangefinder, street-view satnav, image capture, and Bluetooth to my iPhone. "Don't leave home without them!" I'm instructed.

I escape back to the canteen for a coffee—though I could do with something stronger—before I move on to the in-house dentist to have a perfectly good tooth drilled, flat-ground, and capped with a crown containing a miniature microphone and battery.

I haven't trusted dentists from the age of seven, when at infant school, a dentist drilled and filled a cavity after the anaesthetic had worn off, and I suffered absolute agony. He refused to accept my tearful pleading that he was hurting me, and the torture—and on occasion, ridicule—continued until he had finished.

I'm still reliving this memory as the blue-overalled, half-masked and latex-gloved dentist now approaches, and console myself with the knowledge of the Glock under my jacket. "Mr Norton?"

"Y-yes." I say anxiously, thinking suddenly of the British fleet admiral in Napoleonic days: when he was informed there were fifteen French frigates approaching the starboard bow, he told his valet to fetch his red tunic, as it wouldn't show any bloodstains. When his lieutenant then repeated the message "There are fifty French frigates," the admiral additionally asked for his brown trousers!

"Don't be nervous, I've completed this procedure many times and without any problems."

"I'm not nervous," I lie. "I'm the one with a gun!"

The dentist gives a tense smile. "I presume we can proceed with a local anaesthetic—no need for gas?" he enquires with a hint of mockery.

"Local's fine. Just make sure you're giving me enough anaesthetic!"

"Don't worry, you'll be fine." He presses a button on the side of the chair. Its tiny motors give a high-pitched whine, and my whole body tenses as I descend to near horizontal.

All goes well until he unexpectedly hits a nerve. I yelp and jolt my head, and the drill slices across my gum. I sit bolt upright. "Bloody hell," I splutter, spitting mouthfuls of blood into the rinsing dish the nurse hurriedly holds out in front of me. She is young, attractive, and has a sweet smile. But I'm in no mood to appreciate this and glower at the dentist, deliberately letting him see the holstered sidearm under my jacket. I have the satisfaction of him glancing nervously at the butt of the gun before he apologises.

"Sorry about that, Mr Norton. But you did jerk your head suddenly. Now, please lie back, and let's get this finished." I concede reluctantly, muttering under my breath.

Finally, it is done, and I breathe a sigh of relief as the chair is powered upright.

"Apart from that little mishap, I think you'll be pleased with the result," the dentist informs me, removing his mask and peeling off his latex gloves. I ignore him and make for the door, feeling faint and desperate to get to some fresh air. "Oh, by the way, Mr Norton," he calls after me, "I've removed the adjacent molar, as it was rotten. It has allowed me to put in a second battery, so the microphone should last a minimum of twelve months."

I stop in my tracks. "What? You've pulled out one of my teeth?"

"Yes. And you didn't even feel it! It was loose anyway and needed to come out."

"Thank God I didn't let you gas me. I'd be a bloody gummy bear!"

"Anyway, Mr Norton, the additional battery means you only have to undergo twelve-monthly check-ups."

"Wow, thanks!" I say sarcastically.

"It's all part of the service," he says. He smiles at his own joke while repeating to the nurse, "the *service*."

Restraining an angry retort, I grimace, and still swallowing blood, I stumble out.

The anaesthetic is wearing off, my mouth hurts, and I'm mentally exhausted. But I have survived my first day. I head for home, aware I'm going to have to spend the evening going through the latest transcripts from GCHQ. Things are bubbling again, and no doubt tomorrow will hail some new developments on that four-word case (as it's now called): three towns and that weird number.

FOUR

Helen and I have been up since half five, but our bedroom curtains remain drawn, as it's still pitch dark outside on this freezing winter's morning.

As I stand in the dining room, I hear Casper, our boy cat, as he makes a mad dash across the flat-roof extension, leaps onto the adjoining plastic-roofed conservatory, and scrabbles to a halt just before the guttering. On an icy morning, he occasionally gets it wrong and slides headlong into the neighbour's garden, much to my amusement—but to the concern of Helen, who makes me check he's OK.

We've already walked our two dogs—golden retrievers, Grace and Ellie, who enjoyed running zigzags all over the village green following fox scent trails and providing fillings for small, black plastic bags, which in winter I call "hand warmers."

Now, having finally persuaded the dogs to lie in their beds rather than beg at the breakfast table, I walk back to the kitchen, giving Helen a wry grin as I pass her there. "Food belongs to a dog until it goes into the mouth of a human."

She smiles at our shared mantra, checking her no-makeup look in the wall mirror (which takes some time to apply). "Can you refresh the cafetière? And is the toast on its way?" I pause, distracted by the knee-length black dress that hugs her slender figure and her silky brunette tresses, now in the new bob. She'd almost pass as a twelfth-year student rather than an assistant head teacher.

I'm tempted to tell her, but after the usual "I'm always working, never help with the kids, don't phone, could have been killed" grump she was in last night, I don't. Instead, I click the kettle on, drop four slices of wholewheat into their slots, and report, "The toast's in."

Fumbling for a teaspoon in a dimly lit drawer, I remember Helen's continuing gripe about needing better kitchen lighting—"Lots of down-lighters, maybe ten of them," she reckons. It's never ending, the improvements she wants to this house. I've

19

only just finished installing new cherry-wood cupboard doors, wall cabinets, sink, taps, cooker, *and* a black marble worktop—which cost more than the rest put together.

I grab the placemats and quietly finish laying out the dining table—bran flakes, muesli, bread, juice, glasses, coffee mugs, and cutlery.

Helen and I are usually able to eat our breakfast in peace before the girls fly downstairs at the last minute, having fought each other to get into the bathroom. But this morning is different—Daisy appears in the dining room, dressed, groomed, and ready for college—before I've finished making the coffee. "Morning." She gives her mum a hug. "Morning, Pops." My hug is slightly longer.

Helen raises her eyebrows at Daisy. "This is a turn-up for the books."

"It's no big deal. I just didn't want to have to wait for Molten Brain to get out of the bathroom." Turning away to monitor the belligerent toaster, I smile at the thought that it's a brilliant nickname: *Mol*-ly Nor-*ton, top of the class.*

Helen, in her teacher's voice, says, "Don't call your sister that, you know she hates it." Filling the cafetière, I chuckle to myself, which Helen hears. She glowers at me through the kitchen doorway. "And you can pack it in, too."

I carry the coffee to the table and give Daisy a knowing wink. "OK, you heard your Mum. Behave, or she'll leave you to catch the bus!"

Daisy drops her bag next to her usual chair and sits down. Filling her white "Save the Polar Bears" bowl with muesli, she declares, "*That's* why I'm up early—I'm getting the bus."

Bemused, I look at Helen, who also looks surprised. "Why the bus? Helen demands. "Why don't you want me to give you a lift to college this morning?"

"It's OK, Mum. I just want to be more independent."

I am just about to support Daisy when Helen frowns at me and mouths "No." At the same time, the toaster ejects its variously crisped offerings like smouldering lava. The two carbon-like slices I drop onto the floor, much to the delight of the hovering dogs. I obey Helen's stare, pop more bread in the toaster, and put the remaining, least-burnt toast into its rack on the table. I sit next to Daisy, my Daisy. Kids seem to gravitate to a particular parent. Daisy is mine, and Molly her mother's.

We three are halfway through breakfast when Molly swans in, glaring at Daisy. "Blimey, thought you'd overslept," Molly prods, "as I couldn't hear you howling outside the bathroom."

Daisy, with a look of contempt for her teasing sister, snaps back, "I'm getting the bus, *Molten*."

Molly, almost lost for words—a rare event, just like with her mother—looks at her sister with derision. "That's a turn-up for the books, *Dozy*." The taunt merely gets a bored shake of the head from Daisy.

Helen stands up and starts collecting our used cereal bowls. "Right, then," she proclaims, "I'll drop you off as usual, Molly. And you, Lucas, can drop Daisy at the bus stop on your way to the station." *Always* the teacher.

That settled, we all help clearing away the breakfast things, find our bags, coats, and phones, and make our way out to the cars. This is followed by the perfunctory hugs, kisses, and goodbyes as we make our separate departures.

I drop Daisy at the bus stop, and as she walks away, I smile and wave, keeping my concern for her to myself.

FIVE

At Eastbourne station, I catch my usual train and get to the office just before nine. Having sent my report on this case to MI5 only a few days ago, it seems strange to now have their very analysts reporting to me. This morning I will meet them, and their team leader Suzi, for the first time.

Whilst walking along the corridor to their open-plan office, I receive an update text from Coops: *Continued monitoring the world's electronic comms, but our guy has not popped up, and no joy from the trace left on the school's system.* Distracted, and just about to walk through the analysts' office door, I encounter a young woman exiting at speed. With a slight swerve, she just manages to avoid crashing into me.

On recognising me, her accusing stare turns immediately into an apologetic nod. "Good morning, Lucas. Sorry, call of nature. Back in a tick."

Identifying her from her company photo, as no doubt she did me from mine, I call after her as she scampers down the corridor, "No problem, Suzi. See you shortly." I stand and watch her disappear around the corner: a petite blonde, stylishly dressed, running in heels—definitely in a rush.

I remember Jeff telling me, "She has a razor-sharp intellect and a scalpel-like ability to dissect a problem, which to some makes her a little intimidating. And she does not suffer fools." It occurs to me that she could have been a fashion model instead of working for MI5.

Having walked through the open-plan room to my personal office, I hang my duffel coat on the stand behind the door, sit at the desk, and log into my PC. I put the obligatory "new employee" black, leather-bound desk diary and personal stationery into a bottom drawer.

The room is similar to Jeff's, except that I don't have a wall-mounted screen with an attentive Fenella. However, I do have the same black glass table and electronic privacy glass.

The first email of the morning is from Suzi—which has been

in my inbox since 0630!

Hi, Lucas.

Welcome. The team's initial focus is on how these towns are connected, and the consensus of opinion is that this caper relates to some kind of robbery, maybe of a bank or cash centre, but much more likely cash-in-transit. Whichever it is, we believe it's big, with all the hallmarks of a well-funded, professional job. We've established there are no gold reserve centres in Dover or Lewes, although there is a disused one in Newcastle. There are small cash centres in Newcastle and Dover, but nothing in Lewes, and there are no cash-in-transit routes between the towns. Will update again later this morning.

Regards, Suzi.

I've barely read through when the sender bursts into my room like a whirlwind. Before I can stand up, she says breathlessly: "Hi, Lucas. The travel time. It's *possible* by air in a small plane like a twin-engine Cessna. It would get there in twenty minutes of flying time, with forty minutes for loading and unloading."

"*Possible?*"

"Airports. The guys are looking for landing strips near Dover and Lewes."

"Sounds interesting. Thanks for the update."

"I'll keep you posted." Already turning to go, she stops and smiles back at me. "Sorry. I forgot to welcome you on board. Glad to have you with us!" Before I can reply, she's gone.

This kick-starts a new line of investigation, and after only half an hour, she's back. Again unannounced, and bounding into my office.

I look up from my desk strewn with project paperwork and overtime requests and can't help grinning as she clasps a crumpled yellow Post-it note to her chest as she tries to catch her breath. "You OK, Suzi?"

23

She nods impatiently. "The guys have exhausted possibilities and narrowed it down to Hawkinge airfield. There are others, like Manston, which has a runway long enough to have taken Concorde, or Maypole, which is a field. But they are both at least thirty minutes from Dover, which makes Hawkinge the most likely option."

"Hawkinge? I know that part of Kent," I tell her. "I travelled that whole area as an apprentice electrician. I'll check it out and get back to you pronto."

"Thanks, that'll be good, as I've got the whole team scouring maps for a landing point near Lewes," she says. And turning on her heels, she rushes off.

From Googling, I'm reminded Hawkinge was a small airfield that from 1940 was under Fighter Command during WWII. However, after being used for the *Battle of Britain* movie in '69, it was allowed to revert back to pasture. I call Suzi to come to my office, and after a brief discussion, we agree Hawkinge can be struck off the list, dashing our hopes for this to be the Dover take-off point. But she will still get one of the team to check satellite photos, just in case there's a farmer's field landing strip nearby.

I'm still at my desk, trudging through the day's paperwork, when again Suzi runs in to update me. "We've found the Lewes landing point. There's a small gliding club in Ringmer with a grass runway, and it's only four miles from Lewes. I've tasked local CID to check it out."

"Brilliant. Get this wrapped up by end of play, and drinks are on me!"

"Lucas, there's something else. Whilst the guys were doing their research on airfields, another anomaly popped out of the woodwork."

"Go on."

"Well, there's a Dover *Street* in Canterbury. This is only fourteen minutes from Maypole Airfield. It's possible that we misheard the recording and Dover is a road name rather than a town. The same could be said for Lewes—that it's a road, not the town."

"OK. So how many Dover Streets in the UK?"

"According to Google, there are four Dover Streets, four Roads, one Close; and there's also one Lewes Street, four Roads, and one Lewes Close."

"Excellent. What do you think?"

She shakes her head. "Instinct tells me it's a red herring. We're somehow missing the obvious."

"Agreed. And we still have the problem of the source of the cash and the tenuous connection to Rome. Could the cash be coming into the UK from Italy?"

"Yeah, it could just be landing in Dover and transported from there to Lewes, or even a second gang heisting it from the importing mob."

I consider this for a minute, elbows on the desk with my chin balancing on my fisted hands, before I look up at Suzi. "Let's go and have a campfire with the team, and grab a coffee on the way."

Vended drinks in hand, we gather around the team's central carrel of desks. After a ten-minute discussion, it's decided that we need to listen to the original recordings of the mobile phone calls. Suzi dashes off down the corridor to drag David, our verbal communications specialist and truly hyper polyglot, out of another meeting, whilst I nip across into my office to phone Coops at GCHQ. "Hi Coops, how's it going?"

"Fine, you OK? Any movement on the four-word case?"

"That's what I'm calling about. I need a copy of the original recordings you guys made of those phone calls—before you analysed them."

"Sure, no problem. I'll just encrypt them and send them to your email. What do you think you've found?"

"Dunno yet, just need to run through the original recordings word by word."

"Sounds intriguing. Let me know what you find."

"Will do."

A minute or two later, my iPhone pings, alerting the arrival of the email. By the time I've summoned the team back around the central carrel, Suzi returns with David. He is very tall, having to duck through the door. He has a receding hairline, a ponytail, and one week's stubble. He looks like he's been dressed by his grandmother in the cheapest the forties had to offer.

However, Suzi informs me that he can speak six languages like a native, eight others almost fluently, and that his "brainiac" status goes one step further in that he is also a chess master—having won all bar two international championships that he's entered since the age of eight. She also mentions not to call him "Dave"—it was bad enough that the team unjustly teased him on occasion, referring to him as a "cunning linguist." But "Dave" really pushed his buttons.

With the door closed, we all listen to the recording through a PC's desktop speaker, apart from David. He has his Sennheiser headphones clamped firmly on his head, with elbows on the desk, chin resting on his praying hands, and his eyes closed—clearly engrossed. We run through the recordings a few times and then sit in silence, digesting what we've heard. Finally, David breaks the hush. "Did you hear the end of the statement about Dover and Lewes? It's as clear as a bell; there is no interference or missing language. That means they really are both *town* names."

I turn to Suzi and whisper, "Excellent! That means we can now refocus on the airfields." Before Suzi can reply, David calmly puts one hushing finger to his lips. He then replays the sound bites and jots down the occasional scribbled note, insisting he will find something.

The room remains in whispered tones for only a few minutes, when suddenly our now truly *hyper* polyglot squawks, "Got it! I've focused on the Lewes-to-Newcastle connection, and you need to hear the end of that part of the recording. We assumed it was missing the journey's number of hours, since only the fifty-five minutes is audible. But listen again and you will hear a defining breath: it is unquestionably fifty-five minutes!" We all look at him in total disbelief as he continues, "I've flown from Shoreham to Newcastle by air, and fifty-five minutes is impossible."

We're all speechless, utterly deflated, sitting motionless and silent. I'm aware the room is airless and stuffy. Suddenly a hesitant female voice speaks up from the back of the room. "Hi there…I think I've got something?"

Everyone swivels round, startled by the American accent. A petite young woman stands up from a chair near the door, gently rubbing her hands together nervously, and beneath red, fringed hair, bright green eyes dart around apprehensively at surprised faces. I realise she's the "secondment" from the FBI's New York office. The picture in her personnel records does not do her justice.

With a nervous voice, she says quietly, "I'm Elizabeth—call me Beth. I sneaked in ten minutes ago, didn't want to interrupt. My flight was late, then got dropped off at the wrong hotel and—"

"No probs," I assure her. "Chuck in your two penneth."

"Two penneth? Uh…OK…"

"Never mind. Please continue."

"Well, it just occurred to me that by car, Dover is only about an hour away from Lewes." We all stare at her, wondering if she's lost the plot. Seeing the bemusement on our faces, she continues, "Sorry, I should explain. I'm referring to Lewes and Dover in Delaware, in the States. And there's a New Castle about an hour away from Dover."

After a momentary stunned silence, the whole team jumps up and applauds. I bound up to her, past the now-rejuvenated faces, and shake her hand. "Beth, I'm Lucas. Thank you. That's just the tonic we need right now." And then I turn and address the room. "OK guys, follow this up, and use Beth's knowledge of the local area. We'll meet back here at 0930 tomorrow."

I leave the team, Suzi, and the newbie and return to my office, where I ponder the implications of this new lead. It's great to finally make solid inroads to the case, but it's now going to get very complicated with the States, the FBI, and budgets. And my pet hate: intercountry company politics—second only to dentists—bugger!

Finishing the day, I sigh as I clear my desk and brace myself for the bustling commute back to Eastbourne. I console myself

27

with the thought of getting home to a glass of Malbec and the smell of dinner cooking.

SIX

Dinner and the Malbec last night were fine, unlike the atmosphere at the moment between Helen and me—it didn't help that my train was late! Anyway, it's again five thirty in the morning, black as coal outside, and the rain is drumming on the polycarbonate roof of the utility room.

Unspeaking, Helen and I put on our waterproofs and drop the named and colour-coordinated collars onto Grace and Ellie. This morning's pre-breakfast walk will certainly clear my cobwebs after another sleepless night in the spare room and waking with a hangover. But I doubt it will clear the air after last night's row.

With no street lights, everywhere is pitch black, and I imagine we look like daleks with our individual headlamp torches. Grace and Ellie have similar ones around their necks and are now hurtling through the teeming rain like turbo glow-worms. In no time, we're home and breakfasted, and as I put on my coat to leave, I blow a kiss goodbye through the lounge window to Helen, who gives me a hurt, flat smile as she stomps off up the garden in the rain to wake the chickens. I then turn and toss a couple of dog treats to Grace and Ellie—Scooby and Bat-Dog.

Then, with Daisy, we're out of the house and off down into Eastbourne. After dropping Daisy off at her bus stop, I go and get my train. I manage to get to the office at the usual time, just before nine. But I'm feeling guilty at the hurt look on Helen's face when we said our goodbyes this morning.

Although coming to a head now, it has been a long-standing problem in our marriage that I don't "talk about my work"—or much else, really. But it's all part of the gig. The less anyone knows, the better.

I don't feel I should burden her, as she would only worry more than she does already. But at the same time, I can see it hurts that I'm non-committal about my workday with stock phrases like "It was busy, but OK," or the overused "Same-old, same-old. How was *your* day?'

29

It's a no-win situation and has been a bone of contention from our wedding day—when we had to postpone our honeymoon for two weeks due to a case. Nonetheless, that look on her face this morning is still haunting me.

I desperately need a caffeine and a sugar boost, nipping into the canteen for a mocha and an almond croissant to devour at my desk. Just as I sit down, and just as I'm about to take the first chunk out of my croissant, the internal phone rings. It's Jeff. "Did Suzi get hold of you?"

"No…hang on a second." I check and find my mobile is still on silent. "Bugger! Sorry, Jeff, looks like I've missed her calls."

"OK, never mind that now. Your team has pulled together an extremely strong lead overnight following the discovery of our Dover, Lewes, and New Castle being in Delaware. It needs urgent, hands-on verification, which means you and I are going to New York."

"Hell! OK. When?"

"This evening. Heathrow. Sorry it's such short notice. I hope that's not a problem?"

"I guess not. I'll have to let Helen know, and buy a change of clothes lunchtime."

"Don't bother about the clothes, as we'll buy them in Bloomingdales when we arrive. The company can stand that for the short notice. My secretary is finalising travel plans, and she'll let you have the details by noon."

"Right. I'd better get a move on, then."

I quickly finish my pastry and coffee before they get cold. Then I phone Helen. She won't be happy—always wanted to go shopping in New York at Christmas. So I definitely won't mention Bloomingdales! Her mobile rings a few times before she answers.

"So…" She says coldly. "Where you off to now?"

"I wish the guys here had your intuition."

"Well, they would if they knew that for the past nineteen years you only phone during the day if there's some unexpected development and you'll be late, or not come home at all!"

I sit back in my chair, look at the ceiling, and close my eyes for a second, trying to remain calm at the unwarranted derision. "Anyway, I'm afraid I've got to go to New York with Jeff. Flying out this evening, probably a few days, not sure really. Is that OK?"

"Great." And with a barbed tone, "Don't you mind me. I'll look after everything, as normal."

"I really do wish you could come along, but it's strictly business—liaising with their company."

"Really, you wish I could come?" she says with sarcasm. "You know that shopping in New York is one of my dreams!"

"OK, better go, lots to organise. I'll phone when I arrive. Love you lots."

"Yeah."

And with that, she's gone. I don't think she could have been angrier without starting another full-on row. But what does she expect? I know it's not easy for her, but it's not easy for me, either. She knows I can't plan my trips and knows the travelling is always last-minute. I keep trying to understand, but this time, we really seem to be at an impasse.

Jeff and I have arranged to meet at Heathrow's Costa café in the first-floor departure area. I arrive early and find a seat from where I can look down on the plane's preflight preparations: fuel trucks, food trucks, gantries, stairs, and so on. Something I've loved from childhood, like busy worker bees looking after their queen.

The café has gentle background chatter, a regular whooshing of frothing milk, and a queue of people getting last-minute snacks as they wait for their departure gate allocations. It amazes me how many people are business travellers—I thought everyone Skyped now.

On time as always, Jeff strides into the café. He is easy to spot in the congestion of people because of his height and consistent attire. I smile at the way he is dressed: cream chino trousers, dark blue sweater, baby-blue shirt, and Oxford brown brogues: man at M&S.

Spotting me, he gestures to ask if I want a coffee, to which I shake my head. Minutes later, tray in hand, he joins me at my window table. "Is Helen OK about this?" he enquires.

I shrug. "She wasn't over the moon," I admit. "But she'll get over it. She's been with me long enough to know these things happen in our line of work."

Something in my tone makes Jeff give me a sympathetic look. "Oh, by the way, I've sent an email to the FBI giving some background to the case. But let's wait until we're on the plane to discuss it further."

"Agreed."

We swap non-work chit-chat until the overhead signs show our flight as boarding. We grab our bags and make towards our departure gate. Tickets scanned, we cross the gantry into the plane and are ushered to our exit-aisle seats at the front of business class, near the meeting area on the upper deck. Jeff, particularly, appreciates the extra legroom afforded by the gangway to the door.

As we sit, the stewardess confirms that, should necessity arise, of course, we will help with opening the exit door. Jeff and I exchange glances as relaxed flyers familiar with the possibility.

Stowing my hand luggage into the overhead locker, I see two of the massive Rolls-Royce engines that propel this monolith, prompting me to recite details of their invention to Jeff. "Do you know Sir Frank Whittle, an ingenious Brit, was awarded a patent in 1930 for his invention of the jet engine—he was twenty-three!"

Jeff smiles. "Incredible. What would he think of this beast, do you think?"

"Amazed and intrigued, I would imagine."

Just as the seatbelt warning sign bursts into life, I turn my mobile to in-flight mode and settle into my upright recliner. The cabin lighting goes off, as required for night flights, and the plane slowly taxis to the launch point of our designated runway. Then it stops for a few moments as if resting on its haunches, bracing for a full-throttle take-off. Suddenly, engines roar, and the unrelenting acceleration presses the seat into the small of my back.

I look at my Omega Seamaster, my tenth-anniversary present

from Helen. It's nearing midnight, and Jeff turns to me. "In a little over eight hours and three and a half thousand miles, we'll be in New York."

"Yes, a respite for a few hours. Then dinner to look forward to."

"Indeed." He smiles, knowing the foodie in me will awaken. "I think I'll grab a little shut-eye."

"Me, too." I press the appropriate button on the arm of my chair. With a barely audible hum, my motorised seat back slowly declines and the footrest rises.

I manage to doze for an hour or so before I feel a gentle tap on my shoulder. I'm woken by a slim, brunette stewardess smartly dressed in her pillar-box red Virgin uniform. She hands me a padded red leather folder containing a dinner menu listing an appetising selection of main courses, sweets, cheese board, coffees, and wine. I choose the duck in plum sauce, white chocolate roulade, and half-bottle of Malbec. Jeff, as usual, is more restrained, opting for the Caesar salad, fresh fruit, and mango juice.

I guess the choice of meals demonstrates—as if any demonstration is needed—why Jeff maintains a six-pack and I have developed a party-seven. The saving grace, I kid myself, is that my SAS colleagues joked that I'll last longer than most if I fall into the icy Atlantic.

The stewardess soon returns with our lunch. As she walks away, back to the galley, I can't help admiring her shapely legs elevated by bright red, uniform-matching shoes.

The food is restaurant quality, and I say little while tucking into my meal. I love the little details, like the miniature, silver-plated condiment set.

Dinner complete, the stewardess exchanges our food trays for two brandies and a couple of extra-shot lattes. We need to resume discussions on the purpose of our trip, and after swallowing a couple of sips of my coffee, I turn to Jeff. "So, what exactly did you email to the FBI?"

"A summary of the case thus far: GCHQ comms intercepts, the anomalies, and the final interpretation by your team."

"Yeah—anomalies, and a netful of red herrings."

"Are you saying you think this lead is a setup?"

"Dunno. There's just something nagging at the back of my mind, nothing concrete." He passes me a dossier, and I glance sideways to check the occupant of the seat across the aisle is not looking at us. Then I open it. *Top Secret!* I smile, recalling that until the States joined WWII, we Brits used the phrase "most secret." I guess it was more important to defeat Hitler than to educate the Americans.

Through an alcoholic glow, I focus on the enclosed email to the FBI. It highlights the misdirection that has taken us to this point, including information we are still trying to fathom; the number 11210211640553757107735.

Sitting trapped in this Boeing 747–400 flying at 560 miles per hour over the Atlantic Ocean, I can't help feeling this trip to New York has a few revelations on the horizon.

SEVEN

It is coming up to four in the morning local time. The New York-London time difference really throws your body clock as well making the in-flight time seem weird.

The sky is crystal clear, but with dawn approaching, the stars disappear as we continue to descend. Through my starboard window, a lava-like slit shimmers on the horizon, while beneath us, the lights of Long Beach's gridded streets appear to dance magically to the shore.

On final approach to JFK Airport, I watch our flashing red navigation light's reflection glisten across the water of Jamaica Bay. Landing makes the tyres squeal as they hit tarmac, and immediately the brakes and reverse thrust lunge us forward into our seat belts.

Twenty minutes later, we disembark and make our way to the baggage hall to pick up our cases from the carousel. We walk straight through Immigration and Customs, as our FBI counterparts have already arranged full "diplomatic" clearance, and continue straight out to the rank and hail a Yellow Cab to our Central Park hotel—The Plaza.

Jet lag has kicked in, and we say little during the high-speed drive. As we slide back and forth across the easy-clean, industrial plastic rear seats, it's obvious our cabbie is keen to get us to our destination and clock off for the night. After checking in to The Plaza, we drop our luggage in our rooms and go down to the hotel bar to have a couple of double espressos. I make a phone call to Dan Kelly, our FBI field agent-cum-minder, to confirm our meeting arrangements.

Later, just after it opens at 6:30 a.m., I'm sitting having breakfast with Dan in the Cafè Manhattan on West Forty-Fifth Street. He's a stereotypical thirty-something FBI field agent. Medium build, with smartly trimmed and Brylcreemed dark hair, he is wearing an understated charcoal-grey suit and matching raincoat—very Eliot Ness. His choice of clothes makes a statement that he's a government servant, with the saving grace that facially, he's fairly nondescript and would be difficult to pick out of a line-up.

The item Dan mentioned on the phone earlier, which prompted this choice of locale, is this morning's news coverage of the Brink's secure cash centre on Fifth Avenue—at the end of this street. This includes an interview with Brink's controller of security.

The café is a typical old-style joint, complete with large, maroon window sun-canopy and matching covered walkway from the kerb. There's a dining area up on the rear mezzanine and a second small eating area at the front, overlooking the street.

While Dan loads a tray with waffles and a couple of very strong coffees, I nip over and claim a window table just as its occupants are leaving. As we tuck in, he explains that the Brink's controller of security is being interviewed by the national press outside the local SCC (Secure Cash Center) in an hour's time. "I think we should check it out," he suggests.

Dan suddenly stops chewing and gives me a concerned look as I gulp half my coffee, trying to combat my jet lag. "You look beat! Did you get *any* sleep on the plane?"

"I snatched a couple of hours. I'm OK, I can manage on very little sleep. Hope I didn't wake you up with my earlier call?"

"No problem. I was gonna come down and see this new Brink's SCC anyway. Just makes the missus a bit pissed that I couldn't help with the kids this morning."

"What ages?"

"David, two, and Jennifer, six months…" Then he smiles. "Only married *just* over two years."

"Bet that gets the neighbours talking."

"Oh, yeah. You got kids?"

"Daisy, seventeen, and Molly, fifteen—mock-exam stress at the moment!"

"Does it get better as they grow up?" he asks with a hopeful look.

"Yes. Eighteen, when they go off to university! And when my girls pack their bags and depart, I will tell them, 'Leave your keys at reception!'"

"Thanks for that." Dan grimaces.

"Anytime…" And I down a waffle and another good slug of espresso. "So, this new SCC, what's it like?"

"The design is innovative, but like everything, if you know where to look, there are opportunities to get round the security."

"What's so special about the design?"

"It has an open-air compound where the money's loaded by forklift onto trucks."

"Hmm…novel, but risky."

"Yeah. But apparently, the real advances are something to do with their CCTV and a new truck. Word has it that the latter's bodywork material is to be used in our new patrol cars."

"Maybe a reinforced car? Allow for all those doughnuts you yanks scoff."

"Oh, yeah, very funny. Like you limey coppers sit around all day eating cucumber sandwiches and drinking tea!"

"Touché."

We finish our waffles and coffee, settle the bill, and take a walk down the street to the SCC. The NBC film crew is already assembled on the sidewalk outside the compound, surrounded by a throng of onlookers. Looking up, I see the windows of the SCC crammed with employees waiting to watch their illustrious leader's interview. "I hope someone's watching the money," I joke to Dan. But my words are drowned out by a sudden screech of brakes.

A red Prius slides to a halt at the kerb, and a slender young woman leaps out. Dan informs me it's the NBC's roving reporter, Cat Johnson. She snatches a small vended espresso from a member of the film crew, gulps it down, hands back the paper cup, and composes herself. She's wearing an expensive-looking cream summer dress with a delicate flower pattern, cut just above the knee. The high-heel shoes and matching Jimmy Choo handbag.

The controller of security at Brink's, Robert Miller, walks out through a pedestrian security gate and joins her. He is in a dark blue, Italian-cut, single-breasted suit, pale blue shirt, dark blue tie, and brown city loafers, looking the highly paid executive he is. They exchange pleasantries and then step in front of the camera.

Cat takes a few deep breaths and then beams at the lens. The sound engineer counts her in with a verbal "Five, four," and then a silent, fingered *three, two, one.* The recording lamp on the front of the camera goes bright red, and Cat starts her live broadcast.

"Good morning, New York. I'm here on Fifth Avenue with this morning's guest, Robert Miller, controller at Brink's Security." She turns her smile on him. "Well, Robert, we certainly are blessed with a warm and sunny day for the inaugural journey of your new security truck."

He nods and aims a charming smile at the camera. "Yes, indeed, this is a bright start to an important day for Brink's. As you may know, the company was founded by Perry and Fidelia Brink way back in 1859, and we have been the leading innovator in this industry ever since. Today we proudly follow their lead and see another leap forward in technology."

"So, how does this truck compare to those already in your fleet?"

"Firstly, this truck is fitted with a major advance in vehicle monitoring. It has the latest satellite tracking technology, with four hundred sensors scrutinising the vehicle and its occupants."

Cat purses her lips. "That does sound impressive, Robert. But what exactly do the sensors *sense?*"

"Pretty much everything. Each one monitors a specific element—like cab temperature—and it does that one thousand times a second. That data is constantly sent back to headquarters. Sometimes they know what's happening before the driver does!"

"I wouldn't know how you could do that, but I expect even our more tech-savvy viewers are impressed, too. You said 'firstly'—so there are other innovations being trialled this morning?"

"Yes. The truck's bodywork is made from the very latest laminate composite material of glass fibre and grapheme, which is some two hundred times stronger than structural steel—and two hundred times lighter."

With perfect timing, the entry gates to the secure cash centre open soundlessly to give a glimpse of a magnificent, shiny truck. It slowly traverses the compound and parks facing the crowd. "There it is," Robert says proudly. "Three hundred and fifty thousand dollars of massive, high-tech truck." The gates then slowly close just as silently as they had opened.

The camera now focuses back on Cat. "Wow! Robert, that's a big one." Robert blushes slightly, and Cat, realising what she's said, quickly moves on. "I'm also reliably informed that you have adopted an innovative approach to loading the trucks."

"Indeed. We've shifted the loading bays to outside the building, allowing us to have a totally secure wall between the truck and the vast sums inside. It's also easier to monitor proceedings as we load the truck with forklifts, using sealed, palletised containers."

"This is all extremely impressive," says Cat with a fluttering of eyelashes.

"Yes, and that's not all."

She turns to smile at the gathered throng, "Oh really, Robert? Do tell, there's no one listening." And the crowd chuckles appreciatively.

"Well…" He clears his throat. "The most advanced monitoring software is being used for the first time today, and that controls the tracking of the CCTV cameras. The cameras not only automatically detect movement in the compound, but when one of them does, they all track to that same intrusion point, giving multiple camera angles."

"That sounds unbelievably smart," says Cat, wrinkling up her nose and giving another flash of her sky-blue eyes.

Robert pauses a moment and then eases his collar, allowing his arm to brush hers. I wink at Dan. "Any bets as to how long to bedtime?"

He grins. "Right after the interview at this rate—dirty, filthy, lucky son of a bitch."

Robert flips his gaze to the camera, and with an easy smile, he adds, "The software can even differentiate between humans walking or crawling and dogs and cats."

Cat now strikes a feline pose, and the cameraman pans down her svelte figure, pausing at her long, models' legs. "Oh, so it would not see *me* as a burglar, then!" teases Cat. They chuckle, followed by the onlookers as the penny drops.

"You're far too lovely to be invisible," declares Robert, who's then suddenly aware of the lens, hurriedly averting his gaze— which had momentarily dropped to her cleavage.

"You flatter me." Cat giggles and rolls her eyes before adopting a more serious expression, raising an eyebrow. "But, Robert, how did you develop this incredible software?"

"If I told you, you'd never believe me!"

Cat gives another giggle. "I'm sure you wouldn't lie to our audience, would you?"

"Well…" Robert hesitates and suddenly looks a little uncomfortable. "actually, we are not the only company using this type of software. Some department stores monitor the flow of customers and their purchases. That way, they analyse the optimum floor position for products."

"That is truly amazing. So, shopper movements are the source of the software?"

"That's one of its first commercial uses…" He swallows. "But initial development was embryology related."

"Embryology?" Cat frowns.

Robert looks very uncomfortable. "Actually, the software was originally for tracking sperm."

Cat puts on a show of being embarrassed, covering her mouth with her hand to smother a giggle. "Um…well, thank you for that insight, Robert. Unfortunately, we're running out of time, so I want to thank our viewers…this is Cat Johnson signing off and wishing you all a great day in the sun!" She moves away from the camera. Robert follows her and engages in whispered conversation.

I nudge Dan. "What do you reckon? Lunch, then a room?" He doesn't answer, and I realise his attention is focused on a monitor now showing a commercial of a beautiful young couple in swimming costumes running along a sandy beach.

"Jeez, she's gorgeous," he mutters.

As the couple stop running and start kissing, the image fades to a close-up of three small, plastic-wrapped packets on the sand with the strapline "Love. Sex. Durex."

Dan and I start to laugh, then freeze at the sudden ear-piercing scream coming from within the compound. The NBC cameraman bumps me as he picks his camera up from the ground and takes a sweeping shot along the SCC's perimeter wall, down to the massive gates.

I swing round and see that the CCTV cameras positioned high up on the building are all enthusiastically swivelling round to the same spot as the NBC cameraman, somewhere near the main gate. A moment later, the enormous gate slowly opens, and out runs a shrieking girl yelling, "Mommy!" at the top of her voice as she heads towards the mass of onlookers.

Dan and I glance at each other in astonishment, and then instinctively we both run forward to follow her. But she's disappeared into the crowd, and the screaming has stopped. Presuming the young girl has found her parents, we end our chase. I look back at the gate, which has already closed, and then gape at Dan. "What the hell was she doing in the compound?"

"Search me," he says.

"Secure, my arse! So much for their newfangled security!"

We're both a little shaken by the incident and agree we need coffee. Back at the Cafè Manhattan, we find a spot with a view of the TV in the hope that it might provide some further information on the girl and why she was in the compound. Then, remembering the reason I'm in New York, I call Suzi and ask her to check out the truck at Brink's, its payload and itinerary.

After Dan has got our coffee, he sits at the table and fast-dials his head office on his mobile. I listen to his responses. "Yes. Jeez. Yes, OK. Bye."

"So, what's the score on this truck, then?" I ask him.

"It's unconfirmed at present, and they'll get back to me, but at the moment they think the truck is about to carry Brink's biggest-ever cash payload. Destined for the Navy Weapons Station Earle."

"Bloody hell!" I mutter.

"My boss's sentiments exactly. He thinks they're crazy, but Brink's logic is that with the TV coverage, it's the perfect time to show off their new truck and get a free helicopter escort."

"Well, he's got a point."

"Maybe, but…what do *you* think? Opportune moment for our heisters?"

"I don't know. We've been playing catch-up thus far, and at the moment, I'm not convinced we've got the right week, let alone the right consignment."

"Either way, we better make sure. If they do it right under our noses, it'll be a bloody career coronary for you and me." Before I can answer, Dan's mobile rings. It's the update we've been waiting for. As he's speaking, he makes copious notes, including various travel directions out of New York. I guess they must be the truck's routing options to Earle. He closes the call and looks up at me. "Turns out it's carrying forty-eight mil in twenty-dollar bills."

"Blimey, that's a hell of a lot of cash for one base."

"Apparently, some of the cash is for two thousand troops returning from Afghanistan, along with civilians at Earle Navy Base. But the bulk, about forty-six million, is for Shell's Afghanistan redevelopment aid budget."

"What the heck does Shell need that amount for there?"

"Reconstruction work, apparently. They're rebuilding a large area of Kabul. Oilfields, overground pipeline, infrastructure, stuff like that."

"Well, at least we know the amount and denomination; but that's a fair pile of banknotes."

"Yeah, colossal. But it's all accounted for, with serial numbers stored in the Brink's CompuSafe system so they can trace any 'missing' money."

I check my mobile, and a text from Suzi informs me her team's got the same data from Brink's and some background information on the "Aid to Afghanistan" project. I frown at

Dan. "Do you realise that out of those countries donating to Afghanistan, you lot are stumping up one point five-eight billion dollars. I thought you were in a flipping recession."

He grins self-consciously. "We seem to have the habit of trying to be the biggest—even at giving our money away!"

"Well, at least this funding is going via the World Bank." I shrug. "So there shouldn't be any vested interests redirecting monies."

Dan dribbles a little coffee and says indignantly, "Yeah, right, if you believe that, then you probably still wait up for Santa."

"I do," I assure him with a smile. "And he brings me a present every year. He'd probably bring you one, too, if it wasn't for your paranoid immigration guys stopping him."

"Well, they're obviously getting soft lately," he retorts, pulling a note from his wallet to pay the waiter, "seeing as they let you in!"

I make a face at him and quickly down my coffee. "Come on, let's get back to the SCC and find out if anything more is happening."

It is. Just as we arrive, the huge gates to the compound open, and out rolls the shiny, new, dark blue, armoured truck. With a growl, the intimidating multi-bumper nose of the beast swings into the street. It passes within inches of us as it elbows its way through obstinate ranks of taxis, cutting a swathe in the early-morning New York traffic. The rush-hour vehicles jostle each other to move out of the way—and who wouldn't, with a bombproof monolith in your rear-view mirror.

Overhead, the NBC helicopter circles, gnat-like, ever watchful.

I watch the truck move out of sight and then turn to Dan. "Wow! I've got to hand it to you yanks, you know how to build trucks."

"We've failed in one respect, though."

"What's that?"

"It guzzles gas at the rate of a gallon every four miles. My wife has a fit of green rage if I forget to recycle a baked bean can!"

43

"Helen's the same. Separate bins for glass, cardboard, tin, and general waste. But I bet it all gets thrown into one bloody great heap at the landfill!" With that, my phone gets a text—it's from Helen. *CALL ME!* Now, that's downright spooky. And there's no need to shout.

We make our way back to the Cafè Manhattan, and while Dan gets the lattes, I find a quiet table and brace myself before calling Helen back.

EIGHT

It's somewhere around dinner time in the UK. No doubt Helen is juggling between that, the girls, dogs begging, and the aim of getting everything washed up before sitting down with a cold glass of Chardonnay and a soap. The phone rings half a dozen times before it's picked up. "Hello." At home, we all answer the phone in the same way, but from the mildness of the voice, I know it's my Daisy.

I smile as I reply, "How's it all going?"

"All's fine. Do you want Mum?"

"Yes, but make sure it's convenient. I can always call back later."

I listen to Daisy's small sandals clacking across the wooden floor into the kitchen, and then Helen's voice asking, "Who is it?"

"Dad." There's a brief rustle as the phone's passed over.

"Hello. Finally found the time to let us all know you're safe?" She sounds fraught.

"Sorry. It's been non-stop since I got here. But is all OK your end?"

"No, it's bloody not! It's hectic here, and the bloody sink's blocked again—I *asked* you to do something about it *weeks* ago." Before I can respond, there's more. "And Daisy's left her hockey stuff on the bus—I *told* you I should take her to college."

"You did." I say in a placatory tone. "And I'm sorry about the sink." Helen gives a huge sigh, and I take a deep breath. "I know I'm rubbing salt in the wound but…unfortunately… I'm going to have to be here for another few days. Can the sink wait until I get back, or do you want to get Dom next door to pop round and sort it out?"

I hear a yelp, then a clang that sounds like a saucepan lid hitting the floor. "Bloody dogs! Get your paws off the worktop and get out of the kitchen!"

"You OK?"

"Yes, but Ellie has just burnt her nose on a saucepan lid! And

45

don't worry yourself, I'll find the drain cleaning chemicals and clear the blockage myself—if I get five minutes."

"Well, be very careful. Wear gloves, those chemicals can burn."

"Yes. I *know*. I *can* read!"

I don't know what to say, but I can imagine the mayhem. "Sorry, I should have done the drain when you asked."

"So, how's New York?" Her tone has mellowed—the merest fraction.

"A bit fraught. I'm having to sort out a bank problem with the other…company."

"Oh! Oh, damn!" There's another loud clunk from what sounds like cooking utensils. "I've got to go," she yelps, "The rice is boiling over, and the pies are burning in the oven!"

"OK. Do you want me to get the local plod onto the bus company?"

"No. It'll turn up, and if not, *I'll* give them *hell!*"

"OK," I say hurriedly, "I'll ring you tomorrow. Love…" I realise she's hung up and I'm talking to myself.

Letting out a long sigh, I feel guilty I'm not there as backup in the domestic nightmare that is pre-exam, teenage daughters. I make a mental note to buy her something nice from Bloomingdales before I leave New York.

NINE

With perfect timing, having finished my call to Helen, I see Dan strolling over to our window seat with two lattes and a couple of muffins. The nagging feeling I've had since Dan mentioned Shell Development Corporation is building up to a crescendo, and my gut instinct is firing off like Guy Fawkes Night.

Having finished the muffin, and near the bottom of my latte, I grab my mobile and call Suzi. "This four-word case, and the twenty-four-digit number that you're looking into: what's the latest?"

"I'm fine, thank you…how are you?" she replies with a little sarcasm.

"Sorry to be brusque. I've just called home and got another earful. Anyway, what news on that number?"

"Not a thing. We've been through hoops trying to get a fix on it—we've researched phone numbers, bank accounts, IP addresses; we've split it, parsed it, we've had goddamn supercomputers farting bytes all over the damn floor. But *nothing.*"

"Have you keyed it into a calculator?"

"What? Are you in Amsterdam, eating happy cakes?" In the background, I can hear the team laughing at her witticism.

"Have you keyed the damn number into a calculator?"

"Keep ya hair on. No, but hang on a tick while I try and find one." There are now shouts in the background to locate a calculator, a rarely used device given the millions of pounds' worth of computers in the room. After only a minute, I hear Suzi thank someone for a calculator, then a lot of keystrokes. "Right…I've just tapped in *11210211640553757107345*. What now?"

"Suzi, it's something I used to do as a kid and it became known as *beghilos*, or calculator-speak. Basically using the calculator numbers to make words."

"OK. I still don't get it though, what are you on about?

47

What's this Beghilos?"

"B-E-G-H-I-L-O-S—they're the alphabet characters from a segment display—e.g., on a calculator."

"Still none the wiser. I must have missed that decade."

"Just turn the calculator upside down. What do you see?"

"Um…upside-down numbers?"

"Come on, Suzi, group the numbers to make words—like 'hello,' or a date."

The phone goes quiet, but only for a matter of seconds. "Bloody hell, Lucas, I think I've made something!"

"What?"

"SHELL OILS LESSON 911 201211"

"Christ, Suzi, that's today's date—and the reference to Shell—most of the forty-eight million dollars on this Brink's truck that's en route to Earle is Shell's!" I get it. "So, they're going to teach Shell a lesson, and the 911, same as our 999, indicates it's gonna kick off today! OK, you liaise with the FBI techies and get all major cash-in-transit movements for today, and put them on their highest alert. But my money is on this one!"

Dan has been following my side of the conversation with mounting impatience. "Lucas, what the hell's going on?"

"You won't believe it, but I'll bet my left walnut that this truck, or one just like it, is going to be heisted today. Someone's got it in for the Shell Corporation."

"Sons of bitches! I'll call it in right away, and we'll get a team on it."

"And my guys in London will liaise with yours at Langley, so let's grab your motor and follow that truck."

"You bet. My car's not far away." And already running, Dan's on his mobile as we sprint back to his pool car. He gets straight through to his chief, Mike Ross. "Hi, boss. Dan."

"Danny boy, what gives?"

"I'm with Lucas, and he's figured out the target—Brink's shiny, new armoured truck they paraded on NBC News this morning!"

"Hell, give that limey a waffle. I'll get the SWAT teams

airborne. Where's the truck now?"

"It left Brink's SCC at eight en route to the Navy Weapons Station, Earle, so it's still winding its way through traffic, aiming for I-95. Lucas's getting Jeff to come to your office so you can stick him on a chopper."

He gives me a glance, and I confirm with a thumbs up as I dial Jeff's number. "About time you called."

"There's been a development," I gasp, still trying to catch my breath.

"Fire away."

"That twenty-four-digit number! It's a reference to a heist— *today*. And I think we've identified the truck."

"Brilliant. I presume our friends are readying and tooled up."

"Yep, if you get over to FBI HQ, you can hitch a lift with Mike Ross on their chopper. I'm with Dan, and we'll follow the truck." I ring Alex next, our local MI5 field agent, who's somewhere in downtown New York. "Hi, Alex, I expect you've already heard about the Brink's?"

"Yes, got that on the wire a few minutes ago. In fact, I was just about to call you. Where do you want me?"

"Join the chase. The truck's on its way to Earle, and currently heading for I-95. I'm with Dan, FBI, and we're on…" I look at Dan. "Avenue…?"

And he snaps, "Fifth Avenue."

"OK, I heard that," says Alex. "I'll catch up with you en route?"

Dan's in the car and gunning the engine when I jump in and slam the door. He slaps on the blues and twos and floors the accelerator. We shoot off, tyres squealing, and with him swearing, gesticulating, and hooting at dopey drivers and jaywalking pedestrians. It doesn't take long for us to catch up with the slow-moving truck.

The FBI and SWAT helicopters are already circling overhead, along with two TV choppers. The latter suddenly turn away, and I realise they too have received Mike's open-channel, unambiguous warning of a two-mile perimeter with lethal force approval. Any closer, and they will be fired on.

"OK, I'm eyes-on!" Mike shouts on the FBI's secure radio channel. "Listen carefully. Brink's head of security advises they are getting no response from driver or co-driver. The comms system is working, and mics are open; but there's no response. They've probably been told not to communicate. The Brink's guys are also monitoring very high blood pressure and heart rates for driver and co-driver, but the rear guard's vitals are low; he's either not aware of the situation, or he's got a more serious problem. So, all teams hold off and await instructions from me; radio silence."

A few minutes later, my mobile rings. It's Mike again to say he is checking with his comms specialist to see if anyone's talking to the truck—apart from Brink's. As I squint through the windscreen to peer at the back of the truck towering above the vehicles ahead of us, my gut instinct kicks in. "Something isn't right," I mutter.

"What…goddamn taxi!" Dan veers into another lane without taking his foot off the accelerator. "What's that you say?" he asks as we swerve back in behind the truck.

"I would have thought the guys in the truck could give some form of message to their head office? And the condition of their colleague in the rear really concerns me."

"Yep. But the guy in the back might've taken his earpiece out for a nap. It's a two-hour trip down to Earle."

"Maybe you're right. But my gut says we're missing something."

**

It's half nine, and we've been trailing the truck for well over an hour, but still no news or instructions from Mike, apart from him repeating, "Hold your positions" and "Maintain radio silence."

We're now heading southwest on the outskirts of New York, passing Port Reading, still on Highway I-95. Four of its lanes are shepherding through traffic out of the city, with another four serving the off-ramps; it's a huge, sixteen-lane arterial road. Feeling jet-lagged still, I'm glad Dan's at the wheel and not me. I look longingly at the passing gantry sign with a white-on-green exit message and its invitation to the Thomas Edison Service Area. I really could do with a caffeine fix right now.

We've just passed the Exit 11 off-ramp onto Garden State Parkway, when suddenly, Mike's voice shouts at us over the radio. "What the hell's happening? I was told the truck was supposed to take that off-ramp."

Dan wrenches the scribbled notes he made at the café out of the centre console and thrusts them at me. I scan them as quickly as I can, but his writing's as bad as mine. "Mike, according to Dan's notes, that route is correct. It's one of three options, but Exit 11 was verified as today's route by the SCC."

"Do they have an alternate route to the airbase? C'mon, guys, give me some damn answers, and quick."

I peer at the notes again. "The last turn-off is in ten miles— the off-ramp for Highway 18 to Earle."

The radio stays silent. I look at Dan, who says, "If they don't take that, then they're officially off the reservation." Accelerating, he hoots and swears at a driver as he cuts across two lanes in front of us. "Freakin' brain donor!" he mutters.

I clutch my seat belt and dial Jeff's mobile. "What's happening?" Jeff asks.

"If the truck skips the next off-ramp, then my money's on them driving straight through New Castle and Dover and on to Lewes."

"OK. I'll have a word with Mike." Jeff laughs. "It's worth a bet."

Within minutes, Mike's voice booms over the radio, "Now, listen up. I'm set to lose fifty bucks to Jeff if the truck skips the next off-ramp. The upside is that either way, we'll know its destination. So, gentlemen, just enjoy the ride for ten minutes. Radio silence."

Almost immediately, my mobile starts ringing. It's Alex. "Where are you?" I ask, putting him on speakerphone.

"Six cars behind your 'inconspicuous' Buick."

Dan chips in to the open mic. "Jeez, Alex, you're a tricky bastard, I didn't see you hook up on us."

51

"It's my London training, mate; if you can drive undetected in those streets, anywhere else is easy…so, Lucas, what's the SP?"

"If our truck doesn't take the next off-ramp, then I reckon it's headed for Lewes."

"OK, I'll play follow-my-leader—shout when you need me."

Those ten minutes seem to take forever. But, sure enough, the truck continues on, missing the checkpoint off-ramp at Exit 9 of I-95. Instantly, Mike barks at us from the radio. "Now I *am* pissed off, and I've lost fifty bucks! Anyway, probably means the truck's destination *is* Lewes. That's three and a half hours from here, so I hope you guys used the head before you left the office!"

Dan squeezes his knees together and grimaces at me. Then he shakes his head, frowning. "Why on earth Lewes, though, Mike? It's just a little tourist shore town, bottom end of Delaware. Where the hell are they gonna go from there with forty-eight mil in cash?"

"Not a damn clue," Mike declares. "Lucas's team believes there's a Lewes connection and no more than that, but they're working on it. All we can do for now is follow this damn truck."

Dan thumps the steering wheel with his fist. "Why don't we stinger the darn truck and get those guys out?"

"Can't," says Mike. "Bank of America insurers and lawyers, along with the ones at Brink's, want to play this one out. They're concerned about the guy in the back of the truck."

"If they're that damn worried," Dan says, unappeased, "why don't they stop the freakin' truck?"

"Look, guys," Mike continues, "The truck changed routes, so it's getting instructions somehow. It's not from Brink's radio, and our comms team are picking up everything in a five-mile radius, including cabs and pizza delivery!"

"OK…we'll trot obediently behind."

As we continue onward, we identify a couple of FBI cars doing routine drive-bys, trying to ascertain the status of the truck's driver and co-driver. Dan interprets from their hand signals that everything looks normal in the cab. The truck is adhering to speed restrictions, stopping at red lights, and doing nothing that would arouse suspicion that it has been hijacked.

I settle back in my seat and try to ignore my gut feeling that we are being played like glove puppets—some bastard's hand up our butts!

TEN

Three and a half hours later at one in the afternoon, having passed through Dover and New Castle, we're finally on the Coastal Highway. Approaching the left turn onto Savannah Road, we pass a sign: Welcome to Lewes.

As we drive through the outskirts, it shows itself to be a typical, old-style coastal town with pastel, ship-lap timber-clad buildings, neat front gardens, and flower-pot-adorned porches. The occasional modern red-brick structures are commercial, such as banks, civic buildings, and several hotels. There are also many amusement arcades and gift shops targeting the value-conscious, sun-seeking tourist.

Having crossed the town's boundary, I give Mike an update. "The truck's on Savannah Avenue, travelling north towards Lewes Bay."

"About time!" shouts Mike impatiently. "Our blacked-out GMC Yukon XLs are only a few minutes behind you. My fifty bucks are on Lewes Yacht Club."

Dan chips in. "I called the Coast Guard. They'll have a high-speed cutter standing off Lewes Beach in ten minutes."

"Good, but it's *our* bust," Mike snaps. "The last thing I need is USCG arguing jurisdiction just because they now fall under Homeland...OK. Radio silence again. Unless it's my voice or something super critical."

Just after the Wicker 'N' Stuff shop, according to my phone's satnav, the truck should turn left into Cedar Street—the last stretch of road to Lewes Yacht Club. But we drive straight past. Dan grabs the car's radio mic and shouts, "I don't effin' believe it! They went past Cedar Street and are turning right—into..." Dan glances at me for an update and lobs the radio mic back to me.

I double-check my phone's satnav. "Cape Henlopen Drive," I shout into the mic. "It's the northern coast road, and it runs...east."

"Where are these bastards going now?" Mike's voice crackles

back at us. "That damn truck must be running on fumes!"

Neither Dan nor I answer him, as he can see the truck, and we're fixated on its brake lights and squealing tyres as it suddenly turns sharp left into an extremely narrow road signposted "Texas Avenue." Dan slams on the anchors and just makes the same turning, and after fifty yards of tarmac, we find ourselves bumping over a rough track down through the sand dunes towards the shoreline.

Mike again bursts onto the airwaves. "What the hell now? This is a dead end onto the beach." The line crackles and commands, "Pilots. Get me and the SWAT team down to those GMCs ASAP."

Dan quick-fires back. "Drop the birds and GMCs into the Navy Reserve facility. It's just east of Texas Avenue, and their parking lot is pretty empty. It'll piss off those navy guys, Mike, so we'll jump in first and let them know you're coming."

We hear Mike shouting at his pilot, "Come on, get me down there! Now!"

A few minutes later whilst his Black Hawk is plummeting for a stop-go landing, we hear Mike's pilot advising that the truck is now stationary and only fifty metres from the water's edge.

Meanwhile, Dan has turned our car around and is driving at breakneck speed to the Navy Reserve entrance next door. He screeches to a halt at their security barrier just as Alex comes around the corner and, recognising Dan's car, pulls up just behind us.

Dan flashes his FBI badge, demands clearance for us and Alex, and then again floors the accelerator. We rocket across the car park and slide to an ungainly halt right outside the main doors, with Alex pulling up sharply beside us.

Whilst Dan accosts a junior officer at the entrance, demanding to see the base chief, I stand next to the passenger door with Alex, and I look up at the building. It's an old, wooden structure, and immaculate. It's certainly far better funded than our Naval Reserve back home. The main block is two storeys high with several pitched dormer windows, and—as with so many other local ship-lap structures—is pastel blue. In the centre of the roof is a resplendent timber observation tower, which I imagine has far-reaching views across Delaware Bay to Cape May and Atlantic City.

The chest-pounding noise of rotor blades slapping the air makes me turn and look up across the front lawn. Wincing as my sunglasses are sandblasted by grit and grass cuttings, I see the Black Hawks swoop down and drop their FBI SWAT teams from a foot off the ground.

Mike's pilot advises that once the area is secure, one of the birds will refuel at Sussex County Airport sixteen miles away while the other circles the beach.

Bent double, Mike immediately runs to the building's main entrance and takes over the animated discussion Dan's just started with the facilities chief. The FBI SWAT team get Alex and me into their latest black "bulletproof custard" vests and arm us with Glocks. Jeff's standing as moral support with Mike, who has established jurisdiction with the now fully cooperative base chief.

The FBI SWAT teams start moving rapidly along the narrow sand pathway down to the beach, with Alex and me trailing behind. Although unsighted from the truck by the sand dunes, I reckon we must be less than a hundred metres away from it when we hear a colossal explosion.

Plumes of black smoke rise over the sandy mounds as we cautiously run onward and round the final sandbank. The rear doors of the truck are still closed, but the cab doors are hanging off their hinges. I see two guards, no doubt from the front of the truck, staggering up the beach.

The FBI SWAT team grabs the driver and passenger and pulls them behind a dune while one of them radios a paramedic trained colleague. Looking through my borrowed bins, I can see the rear doors of the truck are charred and gnarled from the failed efforts of the first explosive device, but not fully open. A second nano limpet mine the size of a tube of lip balm remains intact on one of the doors—red LED lamp flashing.

Mike has caught up with us, and although only fifty feet away, he bellows over the radio. "Under no circumstances *whatsoever* approach the truck without *my* sanction. I'm waiting for authority from upstairs, so just hold your fire and keep the public at a five-hundred-foot perimeter." He gestures for Dan and me to come over to him. "Lucas, a heads-up: there's a very frank discussion taking place between Bank of America, Brink's, their damn insurers and lawyers, and my boss, the Attorney General. I've told them we're in a stand-off and to damn well hurry up before someone dies of heat exhaustion."

I frown and nod, both to the situation and the politics, and then we all turn to watch the truck. This is now a waiting game, and the clock is ticking, particularly for the poor sod in the rear of the truck—who, according to the Brink's monitoring system, has a dangerously low heart rate.

Dan tasks a FBI newbie to get takeaways, and after only twenty minutes, a crate of burgers, fries, doughnuts, and plastic bottles of cold Diet Coke arrive on the back of a scooter.

Sitting in semi shade behind a sand dune, awaiting the machinations of the lawyers, I start pondering that flashing limpet mine on the rear door. Why had it failed to detonate?

**

It's now been four hours, and I'm still sitting on this bloody sand dune enduring a heady mix of cordite, tarmac-melting heat, and salt air. We've all been involved in this chase for nearly eight hours. The sand is still too hot for bare feet, and we are frazzled—physically and mentally.

The radiating heat of the stationary truck can be felt ten metres away, and its dark blue panels must be hot enough to fry an egg. This temperature level alone could trigger that remaining limpet.

Mike announces over the radio that the driver and co-driver are badly shaken and still receiving attention in the local Beebe Healthcare Center just over a mile away, and one of their paramedics still lingers on the beach, ready for the rear guard. However, that poor security guy remains incommunicado and has worrying vitals.

A nearby SWAT team member unkindly jests that he's like an oven-ready turkey, with his colleague adding "self-basting, if he's sweating like us."

Alex is sitting next to me, and despite being more acclimatised, he's also struggling in this heat. I nudge him and eye-point towards the paramedic. "If it doesn't cool down soon, he'll be dragging *me* off to the Healthcare Center!"

"Yeah." Alex nods. And, rubbing his tired eyes, "After me, you're first."

Looking across the beach, I see a large man in a black suit—seemingly unaffected by the heat—leave the FBI crime scene truck and stride purposefully over to Alex and me. "Hi, I'm Terry Carnegie, head of security for Brink's. Who you guys with?"

"I'm Lucas Norton, and this is my colleague, Alex. We're assisting the FBI."

Terry's just about to quiz us further when his mobile's full-volume ringtone— "The Star-Spangled Banner"— makes everyone look round. The caller takes his undivided attention, and whilst talking, he walks back to the FBI scene-of-crime truck.

I look around at the FBI SWAT team. Despite these stupefying conditions, these black-armour-clad guys remain totally focused on the glinting, twisted carcass of armoured steel. The same team has been listening intently to its radios for the last four hours, poised to launch into action.

Earlier this afternoon, the team's initial recce of the truck's rear got them to within six metres of the remaining limpet mine when its flashing quickened, indicating some form of proximity sensor. Needless to say, they are leaving further investigation to their bomb disposal colleagues, who in turn await the "Go" order from Mike.

After hours of deliberation regarding the Brink's man in the truck and their forty-eight million, Bank of America finally gives Mike the go-ahead. We all jump as he barks his monosyllabic orders over the secure radio channel. "SWAT team ready?"

Their team leader replies. "Eyes on. Area secure. Team

ready."

"Bomb disposal leader—you have a go. I repeat, you have a go."

The gutsiest man on this beach replies coolly, "Disposal team leader here. Moving in."

Peering over a sand dune, I see him slowly move towards the rear of the truck, and as earlier, the limpet's flashing quickens when he's six metres away. He pauses. With so much personal body armour, *he* is relatively safe, but in this case, the movement detector and the hostage within the truck add to the overall risk of the situation.

He's moving forward gingerly, the mesmeric pulse of the red lamp on the limpet mine quickens—until at four metres, the lamp becomes unblinking, almost daring him to venture closer. He continues forward. Then at two metres, the limpet emits a continuous, ear-splitting, high-pitched screech, making us all flinch.

I'm sweating like the proverbial pig as he creeps forward until he's within one metre.

BOOM!

The ground shakes from a thundering explosion. Eighteen stone of explosive expert and bombproof suit fly ten metres through the air, and I duck down behind the dune just as shards of hot metal fly over me. I peer cautiously back over the mound. There is no sign of the bomb disposal guy—he has disappeared into a plume of sand and smoke. The beach is silent; no doubt, like me, everyone is praying he's OK.

But as the dust settles and smoke clears, he becomes visible, lying smouldering like an upturned tortoise. With his arms and legs gently flailing, small pieces of flaming debris drop off his armoured suit. He slowly stands to a rousing applause and bows in response—as much as a bombproof suit will allow. Proving that his sense of humour is also intact, he announces over the radio, "Need more flexibility in this suit. Then I can end with a half-roll and pike finish!"

With that, and seeing that the rear doors now sit ajar with their locks shattered, everyone is ecstatic and stands up shouting, punching the air, and high-fiving.

The FBI SWAT teams split up, with one group moving to recover their dazed, limping, and still-smoking colleague, while the other runs to the rear of the truck. The FBI SWAT team uses large, hand-held hydraulic jaws which, in a single, powerful motion, prise the rear doors fully open…"*No money!*" The SWAT team leader shouts over the radio, simultaneously throwing his arms up in frustrated disbelief.

Given the all-clear from the team leader, Mike, Dan, and I sprint over to the rear of truck. The unconscious guard is taken to the paramedic, who declares his breathing is shallow. But more worryingly, his face is cherry red and lips blue. The rest of the SWAT team surrounds the truck and secures this forensically important but otherwise barren mobile strongroom.

Terry, Brink's head of security, runs over from the crime-scene van and stands between me and Mike. He's elated the guard is unhurt but scratches his head and mumbles. "Impossible. I watched this truck at the SCC. It was loaded, secured, and checked on the weigh scales. In fact, I personally monitored the truck's progress all the way here."

Mike looks at the aluminium pallet and pile of dishevelled shrink wrapping and what looks like aluminium foil. In his broad New York brogue, he spits out, "This…is…not…freakin'…possible!"

From the look of anger on his face, I know better than to say anything, but I think to myself that obviously, *somehow,* it is.

**

The CSIs in their white, plastic, hooded onesies are milling around like albino worker bees. There appear to be two teams, with the first clambering all over the truck, and the second on hands and knees sifting sand to a perimeter of fifty metres. There's a lot of truck and a lot of beach; it will take them hours.

Dan says that when they finish here, they'll put the truck on a flatbed and take it back to their head office for a more intimate inspection. I sense Terry's anguish as he stands next to me, head in his hands, having just been told by Mike that his shiny new

$350K truck is going to be irreversibly dissected back in New York.

Mike gestures for Dan, Alex, and me to come with him to the FBI crime-scene van. It's immediately obvious that he's furious at being hoodwinked by this gang and wants to know if any of the security guards at the Beebe are well enough to be questioned.

Climbing into the van, I think it looks like a blacked-out TARDIS. This thing jokingly called a "van" is in fact a ultra-high-tech RV the size of a forty-seat bus, and as we make our way down a corridor, we're faced by a plethora of wall-mounted and table-surface monitors. At the end, Mike, Dan, Alex, and I sit next to Jeff, who is already ensconced in one of the black leather chairs around an oblong table; even this is a monitor, and it shows a map of the surrounding area.

Mike advises he is calling the lead agent at the Beebe, puts his mobile on speakerphone, and sets it down on the monitor-table.

The tabletop's map zooms in and over to the Beebe hospital, with cross hairs at one end of the building and displaying the target mobile number, which is quickly followed by a picture of the target's owner. Next to that is a list of other available information: relations, friends, colleagues, memberships, and so on. It also lists the owner's most frequently called numbers and shows where those phones are in relation to the Beebe. All this within two seconds of initiating the phone call.

Mike holds a finger to his mouth for us to be quiet. The agent answers, but before he can speak, Mike says. "You're on speakerphone, and the MI5 guys are sitting next to me—how's things?"

"Well, sir, the driver and co-driver are OK, mainly shock. The doc says they're suffering nausea and minor hearing loss from the explosion."

"How about the guard from the back?"

"Far more serious, but the doc's not sure why."

"What exactly does the doc say about him?"

"Hang on sir, I'll grab the guard's clipboard off his bed…right, this says: 'Occasionally conscious. Heart rate low.

Blood pressure low. Significant vision impairment. Major hearing loss. Totally disoriented. Probable cause asphyxia, maybe carbon monoxide.'

"So," Mike ponders, "he's in a pretty bad way."

"When I last spoke to the doc, he said the audiovisual stuff is improving reasonably quickly, but his red blood cells are taking some time to stabilise, especially given that he had a blood transfusion on arrival. His first thought was that the guard fell asleep or passed out with the heat, but like I said, the symptoms make him think it's more like carbon monoxide poisoning."

"Can any of the guards be interviewed?"

"Doc says not for at least eight hours."

"OK. Keep pressuring him, and call me immediately when we can question them." Mike's frustration is rising, and looking at me, he says, "I'm heading back to New York with Dan later. Alex's got his car, so I guess you guys can head off now. We'll all meet up back at my office. " Despite the unappealing long journey back, my heart lifts at the thought of the car's air con.

Shattered, we stagger slowly back up the beach to Alex's unsheltered car, occasionally stumbling on the ever-shifting sand. Distracted by the events of the day, I absentmindedly open the rear door, and the baking heat leaps out at me, making me flinch as the hot air near torches my eyelashes. "Bloody hell." And looking across at Alex, "Wind the windows down, mate."

"Shit, that is *hot*," says Alex as he gets a blast. But nonetheless, he grins as I overtly check my eyebrows are intact. I can barely stand as I watch Alex through the open driver's door window as he starts the engine, sets the air con to max, then winds the windows back up. After ten minutes, we lay our coats on the heat-shimmering, black leather seats and gingerly get in.

The cold air blasts into my face. Bliss! But despite this welcome relief, there is still a huge question hanging over us: where's the bloody money?

ELEVEN

O nce on the open road, I turn to Alex. "First stop—loo. Then some food and cold drinks."

"That's for sure," he replies, and then uses his *Desperate Dan* quote—"I could eat a cow pie." But he adds his own twist: "Chop its horns off, wipe its arse…whole food."

I chuckle, and Jeff nods in agreement, saying, "And some *decent* coffee."

We find a suitable roadside diner just outside Dover, and this time we are able to leave the car under a shady tree in the corner of the car park.

Having used the loos, we sit at a quiet corner table, order from the waitress, and then spend the next ten minutes laughing about the flying bomb disposal guy. Our food arrives, and we each demolish half-pound cow-burgers—even Jeff!

Satiated, we buy some takeaway coffees and then find the shaded and now-cool car. We start the mind-numbing drive back up I-95 to New York. I state the obvious. "If we rule out the impossible, then however implausible, what is left must be possible."

"An old adage…" says Alex, smiling. "But nonetheless true."

"We know the truck left Brink's with forty-eight million dollars…" I continue. "We know the driver was given instructions via a radio mic stuck on his driver's window. We know that when the doors are finally opened, the cash has gone. We're pretty sure the rear guard suffered carbon monoxide poisoning. And we know they drove non-stop to Lewes."

"So, in short, the truck was heisted en route," Jeff summarises, leaning through the gap between the front seats, "as we watched it right up to the time the FBI SWAT bomb squad *blew the bloody doors off*."

Despite his piss-poor Michael Caine impression, we all snigger. Keeping his eye on the road, Alex replies, "But we didn't start monitoring the truck until ten minutes into its journey, so could it have happened before then?"

63

After putting my remaining paper-cupped coffee into a fold-out dashboard drinks holder, I sit back in my seat, frowning. "How the hell do you carry out a heist in broad daylight in ten minutes? We need to get hold of every second of CCTV coverage for those ten minutes, and the truck's black box."

I phone Dan, and it turns out that his Virginia boys have come to the same conclusion. And having determined the precise route of the truck, they're obtaining electronic copies of city and commercial CCTV footage. They should be able to splice together those first ten minutes fairly comprehensively. The race is on—FBI versus GCHQ. I know who my money is on—c'mon, GB!

My brain is in flux when suddenly I have an inspiration— *forklift and a second truck*. I immediately phone Suzi, who answers before I can speak.

"Hiya. I hear the truck was empty."

"You heard right, Suzi…can you get the team to work out how to heist a truck in ten minutes, maybe using a forklift and another lorry?"

"Already on it. In fact, GCHQ have loads of CCTV footage, and some still images borrowed from one of Homeland's satellites!"

"Excellent. Everything OK your end?""

"Yeah. How's the suntan?"

"Very droll! How's the frostbite?"

"Touché. Apparently, snow next week—that'll stuff up the trains!"

"True. OK, see what you can work out, and let me know." I turn to Alex, who's doing bloody well, but his red eyes expose the fact that he's knackered, and it's just him being wired with half a gallon of caffeine that's keeping us on the road. "Alex, I see the office boy has nodded off in the back."

"Yeah. He was a bloody good field agent, but nowadays he's not used to the sitting-around waiting of field work. Amazing how doing nothing is so knackering!"

"True." With that, you can just hear faint snores from Jeff, which make Alex and me smile. I slurp the remains of my coffee and drop the takeaway cup into our rubbish-carrier bag.

Relaxing back into my seat, I try to conjure up an image of two armoured trucks and a forklift in the middle of rush-hour New York. But I can't hold the image; I'm desperately tired.

I want to stay awake, figure this out, and give Alex moral support, but I've been running on adrenalin and caffeine for so many hours.

I'll just rest my eyes for a minute…

TWELVE

I wake with a start when a car horn bellows next to us. Checking my watch, I discover I've been asleep for nearly three hours, and looking out of the window, I see we're negotiating New York traffic.

"Thank God, you're awake." Alex grins at me. "You've snored your damned head off most of the journey."

"Sorry about that," I mumble.

"Don't apologise," Jeff pipes up. "Apparently, I've not been much better."

"I need coffee," I grumble.

"I'll just drop Jeff off at your hotel, and then you and I can drive round to the FBI."

"Need some more beauty sleep, Jeff?" I jibe.

"Too bloomin' right, straight after I've dealt with some unrelated head office stuff," Jeff says, highlighting that it's not only this case he's overseeing. But we know better than to ask.

Ten minutes later, we are at the FBI's head office. "They'll be awash with coffee here, mate," Alex says, slowing to turn into their underground car park at 26 Federal Plaza.

Mike has prearranged a parking space for us, but that doesn't prevent a painstakingly thorough inspection of our car before we are allowed into the brightly lit, white-walled, and bombproof underground cavern.

We are issued with individual visitor photo ID passes, which will be active for the duration of our stay. Then we're shepherded to a lift and informed by a humourless guard, "It will take you right to your floor, and from there you'll be escorted. Keep your ID cards on your person at *all* times, and obey *all* instructions from FBI personnel."

At the lift, I swipe my visitor pass across the sensor, which initiates a staccato electronic voice. "Please state…your name…and FBI…chaperon."

"Lucas Norton…Mike Ross," I reply as instructed.

Recognising my voice from a sample Dan took earlier on his

mobile, the system immediately responds, "Thank you…Mr…Norton. I will transport you to the…twenty-third…floor. Have a nice day…Mr…Norton."

The lift doors open and we walk in. Turning around, I see the implacable basement guards watch the doors close. We exit the lift into a very modern, office-style lobby with hotel décor in relaxing pastel shades of blue, green, and lilac. Underfoot, I feel the particularly thick carpet, which allows ninja-like travel along the corridor.

The doors to the offices are all open, and I can't resist peering in. They all have floor-to-ceiling, clear glass partitions and the same coordinated cabinets and desks as the open area pods: black, red, or white, along with colourful blue, red, green, or black office chairs. The bright colour scheme and general ambiance is the antithesis of our offices back home, as is the silence: ours have a busy-bee hum in the background.

Halfway down the corridor, Dan beckons Alex and me into an equally swish incident room, which looks more like the bridge from the latest Star Trek ship. A dozen eighty-inch, super-slim LCD monitors span three walls; there's subdued lighting at the perimeter and central spotlights highlighting the gathered throng of FBI agents in the middle of the room.

Following a brief introduction from Mike, the spliced footage of the first ten minutes of the money truck's journey is presented across two of the screens. Despite the techno-wizardry, the low-quality images from the poorly maintained street CCTV cameras still look shabby.

Patiently, we slowly trace through the truck's progress, and only for the occasional few seconds does it go out of shot. There are a couple of local agents who know these streets "like the backs of their hands," and they confirm we are seeing the truck's entire progress with no more than twenty seconds' absence from the montage. The truck is stationary at many of the crossroad traffic lights, but for no more than three minutes, and with CCTV on every junction, not one second of these stops is missed.

We spend thirty minutes retracing through the footage almost frame by frame, but nothing comes to light. I'm churning this over in my mind when a brainwave hits me. I nudge Alex. "Is there any way we can measure a weight change in this truck?"

"Yeah. It's a bit 'TV,' but in the film *Italian Job 2*, they took snapshots of the rear wheels of the three lorries, which let them measure the ride height and hence determine which one was carrying the gold. We can do similar, but instead just watch for the truck's ride height to *increase*."

Dan earwigs our exchange, and with my agreement, proffers our thoughts to the room. "Listen up. Our cousins have an idea. Go grab the techies who put together this show and get them to dig out some quality stills at the start and end. If the ride height is different, then I want snapshots from the trip until we find where and when the truck was heisted."

I know this will take a little while, and so nip out with Alex and Dan to the floor's coffee bar. On the way, my mobile rings. When Suzi's name pops up on the screen, I signal to Alex and Dan to go on ahead. "We've gone through the entire CCTV footage," she informs me excitedly, "and at no time do we lose sight of the truck. We've analysed the truck's ride height for those ten minutes, and it doesn't change."

"Blimey, you're quick off the blocks, and you're a step ahead of—"

"Wait. There's more. We have usable footage for the first *hour* of the journey, and the ride height doesn't change; therefore, the truck was heisted later, or at its final destination."

"That certainly puts a different spin on things. Keep the GCHQ guys on it, and if there's any mention of overtime, just tell them it's on Jeff's authority." Finally, I feel we are getting ahead of the curve on this one. It would be great to get a conclusion before the FBI.

I find Alex and Dan at a corner table of the coffee bar with my extra-shot latte. After I bring them up to speed on Suzi's findings, we return to the incident room with our drinks. Dan dives off to the front to brief Mike, who offers me the floor. The findings of my team are considered and discussed for a while before Dan puts a new slant on things.

"There is another possibility," he says thoughtfully. "What if, somehow, they do remove the money, but its weight is replaced," he says, animating the idea with his hands, "maybe a slab of steel mag-locked to the underside of the truck…"

Mike immediately calls the forensics lab to find out if the unladen weight of the truck ever changed—but he's informed that it didn't, and nothing was found attached to its underside. I swear under my breath. Bugger, thwarted again. That's another theory blown out of the water.

Mike calls the Beebe Healthcare, hoping to find out more about the rear guard and the interior of the truck. Neither the chief medical examiner nor any of the other doctors are available to take the call, and he leaves a message for them to ring him back as soon as possible.

Then my mobile rings with another call from Suzi. I excuse myself from the room to take it. "How's it all going? Some more news, I hope, as we are really struggling here."

"Lucas, we've gone through goodness knows how much footage and pieced together the whole four-hour journey. But unfortunately, there's only about thirty minutes of usable ground-level images."

"So, have you found *anything*?"

"Basically, the truck's ride height didn't significantly change during the journey."

"What do you mean, significantly?"

"Well, it did change a small amount, but that could be due to a number of factors: tyre pressures, image quality, viewing angle, and all that. What we're trying to get now are some of the stills taken by the FBI when they first arrived at the scene."

"OK. I'll have a word with Mike and get his techies to contact you. But why the stills from the scene?"

"Basically, the truck slowly gains ride height, but it's only running about an inch higher when snapped by the Lewes Fire House CCTV system on Savannah Road. That's within ten minutes of the truck's final resting place."

"Ah, so the stills from the scene will show the final ride height of the truck."

"Exactly. I'm sure we're right, but how the hell did they get the money out of the truck *on the move*, let alone when it's parked on the beach?"

"Bugger!" I say to myself again. It's not impossible, but certainly damn implausible.

**

The next couple of hours drag with everyone searching through images covering the entire 160-mile journey. I check my watch: 0100 hours here, Eastern Time, and so 0600 hours in the UK. Time to nip out and phone Helen on her mobile. Again, I get the same "cannot be connected" message, and so I hang up and phone home. After a dozen or so rings, a very sleepy Daisy answers. "Hello."

"Hi, Daisy, it's me."

"Hi, Dad, when are you coming home?"

"Not for a couple of days. How are you all…how's Mum?"

"We're fine, but Mum's still at her friend's house in Cheltenham…" and she gives a noisy yawn. "She said you and she need a little space…will you and Mum be OK?"

"Oh, yeah, Mum and me are fine. She just needs a break, and I need to be *there* more."

"That's what she said."

Daisy's poise has always belied her age, and right now she sounds so very grown-up. "Ah, well, let's hope she enjoys her break. Will you and Molly be OK on your own until I'm back, or shall I get Grandma to come and babysit?"

"Please, no. *Not Grandma*. It's all good here, and half term, so we'll be fine!"

"OK. Anyway, you've got Dom's number next door, so promise you'll phone him if you have any concerns, or ring me on my mobile—anytime!"

"Stop worrying. We'll be fine, honest. Love you, Dad."

"Love you too, very much."

I sit in the coffee bar for a few minutes, pondering my work-life balance, or lack of it, before returning to the incident room.

Mike is standing in one corner, shuffling papers. Without warning, he drops the folder with a loud thump onto the adjacent table; everyone spins round, startled.

"Right. The latest information we have points to the truck arriving at Lewes Beach with its payload. This is from hours of CCTV footage and over two hundred still shots." He frowns and, with piercing eyes, glares around the room. "So, how the effin' hell do they get the cash off the beach?"

We're all silent, stuck for ideas. Finally, Dan speaks up. "I still think they could have done it en route, as long as the replacement weight was removed before the truck was reweighed back at the forensic lab."

Just then, my mobile rings. Once again, it's Suzi. I walk out hurriedly into the corridor. "You'll never guess what I've found," she says breathlessly. "This really is *bloody* amazing!"

"Go on. What's the big surprise?"

"I've discovered some more footage. *And*—it's a brilliant view from a new camera installed on the wall of a Bank of America branch. Somehow it's been knocked out of position and is pointing at the intersection. But it's only five minutes from the end of the truck's journey." She breaks off and gulps a breath. "Look at the video I've just sent to your phone and tell me what you see."

Almost immediately, my phone beeps to herald the message's arrival, and I play the video. "OK, Suzi. The vehicles are stationary...I can see our truck at the front of the queue...what am I *not* seeing?"

"Look at the rear of the truck."

"Water vapour from the exhaust?"

"Close, but not right. It's coming from the ventilation grille of the truck."

"I see that now, but I'm still not with you."

"Well, I've also looked at stills taken only minutes before that limpet mine bowled over the bomb disposal guy, and the truck's standing two inches higher than in New York—proving it's empty!"

"OK, I get the ride height, but the steam—you're telling me

there's a connection?"

"Bloody hell, Lucas, this is hard work. Aren't you getting enough caffeine in New York? To spell it out, I reckon the rear of the truck is full of ice!"

"Ah, with you now. Four-hour drive, then four on the beach, the ice melts!"

"It certainly explains the truck's weight changes and disappearing money, but…it also, if I'm right, means the heist was before the truck left the SCC!"

"Brilliant, Suzi. I'll get back into the incident room and let them know *our* team have found the missing clue. I will also get hold of their forensic guys to tell me what the back of the truck was like at the scene. It must have been pretty bloomin' humid, if not awash with water. Back to you shortly."

"Go, Lucas, but stop calling me 'Shortly!'"

As I run back into the room, Mike is saying, "Well, that's it, guys. If we screw around for another twenty-four hours, we'll have fuck-all chance of recovering the money." I make a hand gesture to him, and he nods. "Hang on, guys, Lucas wants to speak."

"Just a quick word. I have an update from my team in London, and I think they've solved the case."

"*Solved?*" says Dan. "Brassy."

"Well, maybe not solved, but it certainly explains how the truck is empty."

Mike gestures at me impatiently. "Go on."

"Well, ironically, the camera that provides the missing clue is mounted on a Bank of America branch." And, like most in the room, I can't help but smile. "But the main thing is that the image is crystal clear and allows a couple of deductions. First is verification of the truck's ride height—an *inch* higher than when it left the compound. Second, we can see *cold* water vapour coming from the air vent near the rear doors." I pause, savouring the moment for myself, and for Suzi and team. "Also, we found a still image taken just before the second limpet went off, which shows the truck's ride height being *two* inches higher."

Again I allow myself a somewhat smug grin. "We believe the

truck was carrying ice, initially the same weight as the money. The four hours of travelling, followed by four hours on Lewes Beach, completes the melting process…hey, presto…the truck is *empty*!"

There is a stunned silence. Then Mike starts clapping, followed by everyone else. "Guys, those limey sons of bitches," as Mike so eloquently puts it to the room, "seem to have worked it out."

"Well, very nearly, Mike. The final piece of corroborating evidence will come from the scene-of-crime forensics team, if they confirm the rear of the truck was awash with water."

Dan immediately picks up the internal phone and speaks to forensics, but during their brief reply, he shows only a look of concern. Finishing the call, he turns to address the expectant faces in the room. "Forensics did notice the rear of the truck was very cold, especially the floor, but it was as dry as a bone."

"So that demolishes Lucas's theory, then?" Mike says, looking at me with disappointment.

"I guess so…" continues Dan. "But they thought the low temperature was kinda weird, especially in the greenhouse-like cabin of the truck. It had run out of gas and had no air conditioning, so the back should have been like an oven. They also say the CME (Chief Medical Examiner) commented that the guard's body temperature was a lot lower than expected, which contradicted the visual symptoms of heat exhaustion."

The room's earlier euphoria is squashed like a bug. I still think I'm on the right track, but my guts are starting to churn again, which suggests I *am* missing something. "I'm still convinced that ice is our strongest theory," I tell Mike, "But I need to speak to the CME about the rear of the truck."

Mike gives me the phone number for the CME, and then Alex and I go to the coffee bar before I make the call. I desperately need caffeine and a quick chat with Suzi.

THIRTEEN

Whilst sitting in the coffee bar, Alex has been extolling the virtues of frappés made with iced Fiji water, and after sucking down a couple of mouthfuls, I agree. But it's a fine line between my craving for caffeine and brain-freeze.

Now, having finished the frappé and used the loo, I phone Suzi. "So how did it go? I bet ya knocked 'em dead," she says expectantly.

"I'm sorry to say that FBI forensics rather dumped on our theory."

"Sod it. How come?"

"Apparently, when they entered the rear of the truck, the floor was cold—"

"But that's good?" she interrupts.

"Yes. But it was bone dry. You're spot on about the ride height, though, so the heist is definitely prior to Lewes Beach."

"What about the CME?"

"Not spoken to him yet, but I'll let you know what I find out."

While Alex tucks into a BLT baguette, I call the CME who confirms that the temperature in the back of the truck was cold. "And the rear guard?" I ask him next.

"He's doing OK. Initial symptoms indicated heat stroke, but the low temperature of the truck and his high red blood cell count suggest CO_2 poisoning."

"What? Like an exhaust leak?"

"Kind of, but to be exact, it appears that he first suffered CO_2 and then CO poisoning. That combination requires a lengthy, low-level exposure to reach our tested toxicity level and still remain non-fatal."

"How do you know it's CO_2, then CO?"

"Simple chemistry. CO_2 is one carbon atom and two oxygens: carbon *di*oxide. But when there is insufficient oxygen, then only one carbon atom and one oxygen atom can combine: carbon *mono*xide."

74

My brain has always struggled with chemistry, but I get the drift. "I won't pretend I understand, but thanks for that." I email Suzi, hoping I've got the atoms right.

Before I've finished my second frappé, she calls my mobile, yet again bubbling with excitement. We're on speakerphone, as I can hear the team chit-chatting in the background. "Lucas, this chemistry lead from the CME is fantastic, and with a slight mod to our theory, it fits *all* the evidence…did you hear that? *All* the evidence!"

"Go on. What mod?"

"You know I said that when we solve it, it'll turn out to be bloomin' simple…well, it *is*!"

"Simple chemistry? That's what the CME said to me!"

"In fact, it is simply ingenious, and that's why it stumped us for so long. We've been running around like headless chickens looking for leading edge, high-tech complexity, and it's just simple physics…well, chemistry…well, both, really!"

"So…what is it?"

"It's bloody dry ice!"

"Dry ice?"

"You don't know what dry ice is?"

I can hear the stifled laughter in the background, but with the jet lag catching up with me again, I am in no mood to be teased. "I know what it is!" I retort snappily. "I just don't know how it's made!"

"You're bloody lucky you got us lot then, and you owe us all a few beers for this one. In fact, drinking at music clubs is where you'd find a lot of dry ice."

"OK! OK! Point taken. How is it made?"

"There is a very simple example. Trigger a CO_2 fire extinguisher into the palm of an insulated glove, and what appears is solid CO_2—which is ice, but at negative seventy-eight-point-five degrees Celsius. As it 'melts'—or rather, sublimates back into a gas—you get what looks like steam falling off the glove. But it leaves it dry: *no* water!"

"So, the rear guard collapses, initially from CO_2, but then depleted oxygen levels give the secondary CO poisoning."

"Yes, and it also explains the two limpet mine explosions with the second one left for the bomb squad. With the time-consuming machinations of the Bank of America, that bought the gang their second four hours!"

"Brilliant work, Suzi."

"Thanks. You'll enjoy explaining all this to the FBI guys!"

"Indeed I will!" I say with delight. This time, I have a real spring in my step as I enter the incident room with Alex. I blurt out, "Guys. The gang used *dry* ice!" Everyone stops what they're doing and turns to look at me in stunned silence. "It fits the dryness and the coldness of the truck floor," I continue excitedly. "And the monoxide poisoning symptoms of the rear guard."

Mike, grinning, bounds forward and shakes my hand. "Jeez, Lucas, awesome news. Now we can concentrate on how the hell they made the switch."

"Abso-bloody-lutely. But, if it's OK with you, Alex, I need to go back to the hotel to freshen up."

"No problemo. I've set a meet with Brink's headquarters guys, so, Lucas, I'll pick you up from your hotel en route. I guess you'll be keeping yourself occupied, Alex?"

"Yeah. I'll probably just hit the minibar and then crash for the night."

Back in my room at the hotel, while I shower and shave, a niggling question preys on my mind. "Why aren't Brink's and the Bank of America screaming at us for answers? Or even asking why our intelligence didn't prevent the heist in the first place?"

FOURTEEN

It's eleven thirty at night as we arrive for our meeting with the head of security and controller at the Brink's secure cash centre on Fifth Avenue.

Mike parks immediately outside, and I stand next to him as he presses the dimly lit call button on the intercom at the main entrance. Once we have identified ourselves, we're buzzed through the main door into the entrance foyer. From here, we are instructed to proceed, one at a time, through the rotary access door situated at the opposite side of the room.

This RAD comprises two upright steel tubes, one inside the other. The unmoving, outer tube is fixed into the wall and has two opposing doorway cut-outs. The inner tube has only one doorway cut-out and rotates to align with one or the other in the outer tube. If the system determines a problem, then the inner door stops between the outer doorway cut-outs, preventing egress, and raises an alarm. Heaven help the claustrophobic!

Mike gestures for me to enter first. I step in, and the inner door slowly turns ninety degrees and stops. It seems to take an age for the system to determine my physical statistics: height, weight, face recognition, eye and hair colours, and skin pigment are scanned and recorded. The inner door then unhurriedly rotates a further ninety degrees, and I jump out into the main hallway. If any of my physical statistics change while I'm in this building, then I won't be leaving in a hurry.

While I wait for Mike to join me, I can't help smiling as I recall a similar incident. Many years ago, a colleague of mine who had broken his wrist over the weekend was let into an SCC by a co-worker smoking outside an unlocked fire door—totally forbidden. But later that day, when my plaster-cast colleague went to leave through the rotary access door, the system compared him to his last-known, non-plaster-cast weight and initiated a lockdown. If it hadn't been so funny, both guys would have been sacked.

But at this SCC, I realise security is taken far more seriously as four armed guards meet us at the reception desk and put us through an airport-level security scan. However, on seeing Mike's badge, they wisely refrain from taking our phones or his sidearm. They escort us past a canteen, a restroom, and then into a lift and up to the fourth-floor managers' offices, where the décor changes from bombproof utilitarian to pampered executive.

We are met by Terry, head of security, and Robert, the controller, in the executive boardroom. They are dressed far more casually than when I last saw them: Robert at the NBC News interview, and Terry on the beach at Lewes. This time, jeans and Ts are the order of the day.

After we all shake hands and introduce ourselves, Robert gestures to the dresser. "Can I interest you guys in coffee and a sandwich?"

"Thank you," I reply, as we all walk to the side table. "It's been a long day." I'm tempted to tell Robert that we were present at his NBC News interview and enjoyed the repartee with his interviewer, but I decide it's better not to under the circumstances and focus instead on the buffet.

With our small plates of finger food and mugs of coffee, we adopt the usual team positions on opposite sides of the oval, teak table and sit down in the dark oxblood leather chairs. After carefully aligning his Waterman pen one inch from the side of his leather-bound pad, Robert leans back and kicks off the meeting.

"So…," he says, looking at both of us, "how's the case progressing?"

I leave it to Mike to answer, as it's his jurisdiction. And, in any case, I'm still wolfing down a BLT sandwich. "I believe we know how the truck came to be empty, and why that particular route."

Terry scribbles a note on his cheap, comb-bound pad and, twiddling his biro, joins the conversation. "Nice work, Mike. Can you give us a layman's synopsis?"

"They replaced the cash in the truck with its equivalent weight in dry ice." Mike replies. "The four-hour journey, plus four hours on Lewes Beach, melts the dry ice, and hey, presto—empty truck!"

"How did they know they'd get the second four hours?" Robert asks, repositioning his pen.

"They didn't. But…they did understand that the second limpet mine, along with your rear guard being unconscious, would initiate your legal deliberations."

Terry clasped his hands on his notepad. "If that's the case, then why was this meltwater not picked up by the FBI sooner?"

I smirk slightly; they think the FBI missed a trick.

"There was no meltwater," Mike says authoritatively. "Dry ice is made from CO_2, which doesn't melt. It sublimates." And with hands gesturing smoke rising. "It turns from a solid right into a gas. A stroke of genius, frankly, since the fumes knocked out your guard."

Terry's brow furrows. "OK. So…when did they replace the cash with the dry ice?"

Mike motions for me to answer. "That's the main reason we're here." Looking at Robert, I say, "We have CCTV footage proving that the truck did not stop on its way to Lewes beach…" and, moving my gaze to Terry, "you were there. The transfer could not have taken place on the seafront…"

"What are you saying, exactly?" demands Terry frustratedly.

Then, glancing at them both, I continue. "It *must* have happened *before* the journey commenced."

Robert and Terry look at each other in disbelief. Then Robert looks at me, shaking his head. "No! No way!" he says vehemently, "you're not palming this onto us. We can prove the cash was secure in the truck when it left the compound."

You can cut the air with a knife. Both of them are sitting back in their chairs, arms folded and glaring at Mike…then me…then Mike. We all sit quietly for a minute, sipping our drinks, letting passions wane a little. I lean forward, hands open on the table.

"We have no intention of passing the buck," I say with a placating sigh, "but we must establish the facts. All we are saying is that during its journey, the truck had more eyes on it than the Pope on inauguration day, and therefore, we must now determine how the ice-for-cash exchange could be done within your SCC. To do this, we need to scrutinise your CCTV footage for that consignment."

"Now? You want to review it right now?" Terry asks.

"Yes, please." I nod.

Terry briefly whispers to Robert, then picks up the phone and instructs one of their techies to come up to the boardroom and run through their footage of the morning. Within a few minutes, we are all watching earlier CCTV on a massive screen. It's clear that Terry runs "his" SCC like a military operation.

The first ten minutes of the recording shows the money being counted, double-checked, and manually stacked into secure, stainless steel mobile vaults, which are reminiscent of very shiny, two-drawer filing cabinets. These are then secured to a stainless steel pallet. After that, the whole thing is wrapped in what looks like industrial cling film. "That stuff is obviously stronger than Christmas wrapping paper," I joke, trying to lighten the mood.

"You better believe it." Terry smiles. "You'd need more than a shiv…it's self-amalgamating, watertight and tamper-proof." We now watch a forklift with the pallet drive to the closed external security doors, at which point the recording jumps to an external camera and a view of the truck as it reverses across the yard.

Suddenly, the compound's main gates open, and the shiny new lorry is on open display to the media and public gathered on the sidewalk. We can see Robert doing his interview with NBC, proudly gesturing at his shiny, new truck. There is even a glimpse of Dan and me in the background just before the gates close.

The screen now shows the external security shutters opening and the forklift driving out across the compound to deposit the money ten feet behind the truck. The rear guard opens the back doors, climbs aboard, and gives a thumbs up for the pallet to be loaded. The empty forklift returns into the main building, with the security shutters closing behind it.

Almost immediately, the truck drives over onto the weigh station, where its weight is verified, and then on to the main entrance gate, which slowly opens. The truck moves off into the street to start its journey: one hundred and sixty miles. The compound gates close, and the CCTV footage moves to the front of the building, where we see the truck negotiate the busy New York traffic.

Mike clunks his coffee mug down in frustration. "Jesus, are they effin' magicians?"

"Hang on a minute," I blurt out. "Something's not right. Terry, please would you replay the footage…? From the pallet being placed behind the truck." We watch again, and I focus on the time-stamp of the footage. And there it is. I point out a six-minute gap between the pallet being dropped behind the truck and it being loaded.

Robert and Terry sit back in their chairs, looking sheepish. Terry clears his throat. "*We* removed that footage. It's irrelevant to the case. But it does show a potential problem with our security processes. It's not something we want to share with the public or our largest client—Bank of America."

Mike's anger rises, and I wait for the mug to disintegrate in his white-knuckle grip. He glares at Robert. "We are not the goddamn 'public!'" he exclaims. "We need to see that damn footage…now!"

"Show the original…" Terry demands of the techie. The poor guy nervously closes the first file, navigates on screen to another, hits *play*, and fast-forwards to a time approximately thirty seconds before the missing footage of the prior file. This time, six cameras are on screen concurrently and all monitoring the compound, including its security shutters, main gate, truck, and forklift.

Mike and I sit stock-still, focused on the screen. Suddenly, as we reach the start of the gap, we see the driver, co-driver, rear guard, and the forklift driver all rush towards the compound's main entrance. Simultaneously, all six cameras track them across the yard and zoom in on them and a child who appears to be pounding on the main gate.

The driver runs over to the gate's lock override keypad and appears to take several attempts to enter the unlock code correctly. Finally, the gate slowly starts to move. The child squeezes through the gap and races out into the crowd. The six CCTV cameras remain focused on the entrance as the TV crews frantically wield their cameras and the presenters badger the guards for answers.

The driver punches the bright red button on the controller, and the gates slowly close. The CCTV cameras return to their original monitoring positions, and we see the guards and forklift driver walk back to the truck. We now rejoin the earlier footage, where the truck's back doors open, the guard climbs in to confirm all is clear, and the pallet loaded.

Robert tells the techie to stop the playback and return to his office. We sit contemplative for a minute before I look at Terry and break the uneasy silence. "I presume you see the problem?"

"Yes. None of the guards remain with the truck," he replies, sounding frustrated. "They'll be undergoing stringent refresher training over the next few days."

"The guards?" Mike says, exasperated. "They're the *least* of your problems." Robert and Terry swap quick, nervous, glances and then look at Mike, eager for an explanation. "The CCTV system!" Mike continues angrily. "It had all six cameras tracking the guards and the situation at the gate, leaving the truck completely unmonitored for more than five minutes. Please tell me you have some other footage or staff monitoring that damn truck at the time?"

Terry looks shamefaced; this brand-new CCTV system is his baby. "No. I'm afraid not." He sighs. "In fact, we were far more concerned with the possibility of the mother's lawyers suing us for negligence."

After some discussion, Robert and Terry give us a copy of the complete footage on a memory stick, and we thank them for their hospitality. We must now get all CCTV footage from the surrounding area—especially from the TV news crews; their cameras had been facing the compound.

Mike gets his team onto tracking down the TV footage using the personal contacts he has with most of the channels. I give a similar brief to my team in London. Suzi will also get some satellite footage as, due to an unrelated security matter, one of our satellites was retasked to pass over New York as a favour to Homeland.

Mike and me are off and running, literally, as we try to make our appointment with David and Barbara at the Bank of America Tower at One Bryant Park. I certainly hope it goes easier than the meeting we've just had with Brink's. The jet lag is raising its ugly head again, but this brief dodgem ride with Mike across central New York should keep me alert—brace yourself, stomach.

FIFTEEN

It's nearing 1:00 a.m., and Mike and I stand outside Bank of America's main entrance. I realise I've seen this vista before: Times Square. The opulence of money is everywhere. And, at twelve hundred feet, they have one of the tallest buildings in New York. "How the other half live," I say to Mike.

"True…and in a recession," he replies resentfully.

As we walk across the massive, cream-marble-floored reception area, we're in surroundings that are quite literally spectacular. The high ceiling has large, ornate cornicing, huge, gilded, glittering chandeliers, and walls of beautiful frescos and porticos that would not look out of place in Venice.

We are here to see the *grands fromages* of the bank, who've just flown in from their headquarters in North Carolina and no doubt expect answers from us rather than the other way round. Barbara is a director and member of the bank's audit committee and enterprise risk committee. David is their chief executive officer, and a director.

At the reception desk, we sign in, clip on our visitor passes, and walk through an archway-style, full-body scanner. A note is taken of Mike's weapon and our phones; as at Brink's, we don't relinquish them. After making an internal phone call, a burly private security guard informs us that "David's PA is waiting," and then he accompanies us to one of the fifty-two lifts, which whisks us to the executive suite.

When the lift doors open on the fifty-third floor, we are met by a tall, auburn-haired lady. She is smartly dressed and has a small brightly coloured hibiscus brooch on her jacket collar. "I'm Jackie, personal assistant to David," She says with an air of restrained confidence. "Welcome to our offices. May I get you a drink?"

"A double-shot latte, please." I reply.

"Same here," Mike agrees.

"No problem. I'll take you to David and Barbara in the boardroom," she advises.

As we enter the room, David stands up from his chair. "Welcome. This is Barbara, I'm David. Please, take a seat." We all make ourselves comfortable in the sumptuous cream leather chairs that match the light oak table. In front of Mike and me are a couple of notepads, pens, and our host's business cards. All are adorned with the bank's slogan: "Life's better when we're connected." This makes me smile as I recall the Brink's truck's radio problems.

"Mike, FBI…" and gesturing to me, he adds, "and this is Lucas…MI5."

David smiles cordially and looks at Mike. "Can you give us a précis of the current situation?"

"Yep, but firstly…thanks for meeting us." And, raising his eyebrows, "particularly as you had to fly in at this unholy hour." Barbara and David nod politely to Mike's gratitude, and then he continues. "I presume you're aware we believe the heist occurred before the truck left the SCC?"

Barbara sits back gently in her leather seat, looking at Mike. "We are. We got a call from Brink's a little while ago. However, we too found a couple of anomalies and are double-checking our serial number database."

I interject. "What do you mean, anomalies?"

She switches her smile from Mike to me. "I await final confirmation, but one of our branches appears to have processed a stolen twenty-dollar bill. It was left in their overnight drop box and is part of the day's takings at a local coffee house."

Mike and I look at each other, flabbergasted. "*If* this is correct…" I say in a disbelieving tone, "we are dealing with very confident, if not downright cocky individuals."

There's a tap on the door. "Come in," calls David.

Jackie appears with our drinks in fine china crockery, along with a plate of fancy chocolate biscuits. She then leaves, and the door clicks shut behind her.

Mike looks at Barbara. "How long before your guys clarify if this bill is part of the heist?"

"A scanned image of the bill should reach us by email any minute," she replies, "and the original will be couriered here.

You might be able to get forensic evidence from it."

At that moment, David's mobile pings. He looks at it and then nods to Barbara. "It's here." And then leaning across the table, he presses the intercom button. "Jackie, please, could you return to the boardroom and put Barbara's email on the wall monitor?"

Within minutes, Jackie is sitting in the chair next to David. She double-taps a specific point of the table top, which instantly transforms into a touchscreen keyboard. Another couple of taps, and an email appears on the LED screen on the wall. A $20 bill is clearly visible, and she zooms in to the bright red ellipse drawn around its serial number.

Jackie then overlays another document on the screen. This lists dozens of bill serial numbers in the Brink's consignment. Two thirds of the way down, a line is highlighted with another red ellipse: the same serial number. Barbara leans forward. "As you can see, the bill *is* from the heist."

We've been chatting generally for only a few minutes when the call-conferencing unit in the centre of the table buzzes, and David nods to Jackie to answer it. "Jackie here."

"Hi, this is the front desk. I have an urgent package for you."

"Excellent," Jackie replies. "Please have someone bring it to the executive floor—I'll meet them at the elevator." And with that, she leaves the room.

A few minutes later and Jackie returns, handing the Jiffy envelope to David. He checks the contents and then slides it across the table to Mike. "Please let us know how your forensic guys do."

"I'll call you as soon as I know more," Mike replies and excuses us.

Whilst driving back to the FBI forensics lab, I update my team in London, who are equally gobsmacked by the appearance of this $20 bill.

SIXTEEN

I leave Mike in his office to deal with his forensic team and head to the now-empty coffee bar—it is 2:00 a.m.—in the hope of grabbing a desperately needed forty winks.

I've barely settled myself across a leather sofa when Suzi's number vibrates the crap out of my otherwise silent mobile. "Sorry it's so late, or early…where are you?"

"In the coffee bar at FBI HQ," I reply whilst remaining prostrate and barely stifling a yawn.

"Oh. Thought you'd be back at your hotel," she says, distracted. "Anyway, good news…and some not-so-good news…which do you want first?"

"Any way you like…" This time I'm unable to stop a yawn.

"You need to get some sleep."

"You think?" I say grumpily. "Go on. Let's see what you've found."

"Well, the mobile we've been monitoring since it was in Berkley Square, London, has fired up and sent a text to northern Italy. Not only that, but it's a hundred miles or so north-northwest of New York."

I sit up so quickly I damn near faint. "Bloody hell…fantastic! What's the text say?"

"It's just another flippin' number – I'll text you the thirteen characters."

"OK, I'm going to get a coffee." While the bean-to-cup machine grinds and hisses, my phone vibrates. I look down at the message—*9903533453379*—which when upside down *could* be GLEESHEESEDGG. "If it's like the last one, we'll have to split it up into words."

"That's what we're doing, but the kids here are becoming fractious."

"Transfer me to the conference unit." There's two seconds of silence; then suddenly, I can hear everyone much clearer. "Hi to all of you FBI beaters!" I shout, which gets a roaring cheer. "So, what are your thoughts?"

87

"I think it's either some form of text shorthand or slang," shouts David, our cunning linguist. "It certainly isn't any language I recognise."

Then Suzi. "I could send the number to my young niece, Anna. She spends most of her waking hours on social network sites, Facebooking, texting, tweeting, etcetera."

"Nice one. It's just gone 2:00 a.m. here but breakfast there, so do it now."

I hear her in the background calling her niece and texting the number. Meanwhile, the rest of us continue to explore different avenues, which unfortunately all turn into cul-de-sacs. After a few minutes, a mobile rings. "It's my niece!" shouts Suzi. "I'll transfer her to the conference unit."

A child's voice now joins us. "Hello…" she says tentatively, "I'm Annabel."

"Hello, Annabel. I'm Lucas. I work with your auntie. So…have you managed to solve our puzzle?"

"I'm not sure… I think the message is three words: *glee sheesed G6.*"

"Sorry, Annabel, I don't understand…what do these words mean?"

"The first two are slang. *Glee* means happy, and *sheesed* is maxed out. I'm guessing that your GG could be *G6*…for the G650 Gulfstream aeroplane. It's trending really high, with its faulty engine problem."

Silence. The team and I are dumbstruck.

After a few seconds, the shy voice enquires, "Hello?"

"Sorry, Annabel. That is fantastic!" I enthuse. "I didn't consider the last character being a six. I'm sorry, but your solution means I need to dash and do a lot more work. Thanks for your help."

Suzi agrees to call her niece back in a while to finalise a treat; apparently an iMax movie and KFC are the order of the day. "She certainly earnt that treat!" Suzi says with pride.

"Abso-bloody-lutely," I agree. "Pass her details on to HR."

"Lucas…" Suzi says confidently, "They're probably flying the money out from near to where that message originated."

"Agreed. But we need a specific—"

And at that point someone in the team interrupts me. It's Bernard. "I've found a small airport at Monticello, north upstate New York. It's very close to our phone fix. Closed in 2006, but up until then, it served aircraft like the G6."

"I'll get this intel to the FBI so they can get a team out there," I say excitedly. "Let me know if those mobiles fire up again, Suzi!"

I immediately phone Mike and give him the good news. He's cock-a-hoop and tells me to meet him in his office. I down the last mouthful of my coffee and go find him.

**

I stand in Mike's office and listen to him on his phone scramble three FBI choppers for Monticello's former airport. Then he calls the Monticello Police and tells them what's happening—and to "keep out of the damn way," which doesn't need repeating with FBI and SWAT turning up airborne!

I leave Jeff and Alex to hold the fort in New York and accompany Dan and Mike in what feels like his personal Black Hawk. Once in the air, I browse the web on my iPad to find information about the Gulfstream and its flying time and hopefully an insight into the gang's flight plan options.

Finally, I feel we are gaining some ground in tracking them down.

When the navigator sees me googling G6 data, he advises over the radio, "Don't forget, flight distances are in nautical miles."

"What difference does that make?" I query.

"A nautical mile equates to one minute of arc of latitude at the equator, or 1.15 miles, or 1.85 kilometres—take ya pick."

I smile politely. "I'll just treat them as miles, that'll be near enough." Interestingly, I discover that the Rolls-Royce powered G650 Gulfstream is the fastest and yet longest-ranging business jet, and it has a take-off distance of five thousand five hundred feet: just under the length of Monticello's runway. What is more noteworthy, though, is it has a limit of seven thousand nautical miles at 0.85 mach, and it can cruise at fifty-one thousand feet. This means the G6 can do the 6,940-nautical-mile round trip from New York to London with one tankful. Or fly one-way to Paris, Rome, or even Dubai.

With the Black Hawk flat out at 185 miles per hour, we near Monticello only thirty-five minutes after leaving the rooftop helipad of FBI Plaza. Through my helmet's headphones, I hear Mike's instructions to the pilot. "Come in low and quiet over the trees from the south, and put us down on the access road in front of the hangars."

"Roger that," replies the compliant pilot, adding, "The northerly breeze will also help mask our approach." The ex-navy pilot topiaries the tops of the trees and drops us rapidly but gently onto the ground. The other two Blackhawks perform the same trick, landing either side of us.

The SWAT teams disembark, crouching like armoured ninjas. Moving swiftly and silently, they surround the hangars and cut off the escape for anyone inside.

As Mike and I run across the taxiway to other outbuildings, we catch sight of a plane thundering down the runway, engines full-chat, straight at us. Mesmerised like a rabbit in headlights, my heart is near pounding out of my chest when, suddenly, just in time, the nose wheel lifts and the plane rockets overhead, bowling me over with the jet wash. I roll onto my back and look skyward to see its undercarriage clip the treetops and disappear rapidly southward.

Mike, also blown off his feet, and now with an expression like an enraged grizzly, brushes gravel from his palms and shouts at the top of his voice, "Bastards…!" And, accentuating every word, "One effin' step behind again. I'm not standing for this bullshit!" He then turns around to face the choppers and bellows over the radio. "Put out a call to Homeland Security advising that a suspected terrorist plane is flying south from Monticello. It *must* be grounded before it reaches New York."

Through my earpiece, I listen to the pilot putting out the call, knowing all hell will now break loose. Within thirty seconds, the flight leader of three formidable F16s which were patrolling over New York City replies that he's now en route to intercept the little G6.

A replacement F16 is already in the air from Hancock Field Air National Guard base at Syracuse, about two hundred and fifty miles north-northeast of New York to replace him and join the remaining two he left circling the city.

A minute later, the Homeland Security director's voice echoes over my earpiece, authorising the flight leader to use deadly force. This is broadcast both on our secure channel and on the commercial frequency of the G6.

Mike turns to me. "That'll scare the crap out of the bastard." And within seconds, the radio waves are crackling with the G6 pilot's total compliance, asking where we wish him to land. Strangely, despite three minutes of crystal-clear instruction from the F16 flight leader, the G6 flies unswervingly on towards New York. I can feel the blood slowly draining from my chest.

Every move of both the G6 and the F16 flight leader is repeated over the radio so that Homeland is kept up to date verbally, as well as by their all-seeing satellites. Then the F16 flight leader announces he is executing a very slow flypast, gently rolling the F16 to show the G6 crew its colossal underbelly armoury. But still there is no change in the G6's flight path. Its pilot continues to say that he's changing course, but the plane carries on towards New York.

Homeland Security assesses the situation as "outside the permissible response envelope" and instructs the F16 flight leader to initiate missile lock-on, followed by confirmation to the G6 pilot that he will fire. The two planes are now seven minutes from central New York and nearing the end of open countryside.

The F16 flight leader initiates missile lock-on and advises he *will* fire if the G6 does not turn back within ten seconds. The pilot of the G6 is now screaming his obedience, but the plane does not alter its flight path one single degree.

The F16 flight leader hesitates and gives one more warning to the G6 pilot that he will fire if compliance is not forthcoming *immediately.* The G6 pilot is now shrieking virtually unintelligibly into his microphone. But, relentless, his plane continues its path.

We hear the final, unambiguous, and irrevocably chilling words: "Homeland. This is F16 flight leader confirming fire order."

"This is Homeland," a voice replies impatiently. "Fire order reconfirmed!"

I hold my breath.

"Lock-on affirmed," says the F16 flight leader impassively. "Firing…missile away."

Then, a few seconds later, over the radio we hear a massive explosion, followed by chilling words from the F16 flight leader. "Target destroyed. Coordinates transmitted for ground crew recovery… F16 returning to base. Out."

So quick. So ruthless. So…permanent.

I feel a sickening loss and walk over to the grass verge, bend down, and throw up.

Mike looks at me, concerned. "Christ, Lucas. You going soft in your old age? They pissed on the eagle's head, and it ripped off their balls!"

"Bloody hell, Mike. Innocent people may have died here!"

"Come on, Lucas, be logical. Who in their right mind would be shown the underbelly of a city-destroying F16, let alone hear the warning of a lock-on, and then totally freakin' ignore it?"

"Normally, I would agree. But why was the pilot screaming compliance, yet the plane stayed on course, especially when he *knows* he's going to be blown into a million pieces?"

"He was just buying time, hoping we would back down and try negotiating. But the Homeland and the FBI don't effin' negotiate. Not after 9/11. We just fucking *don't!*" I leave it at that. There's no point arguing—we may both be agents of our states, but we have been raised in different worlds.

We get back to the choppers and quickly pack up our gear, but I'm in a far more sombre mood than the FBI SWAT teams who celebrate with high fives as if they just won a game of baseball. That's where our agencies differ. As my dad always said, "The FBI are like Dobermanns seeing another dog—either fuck it or fight it!" MI5 want to find the root cause, striving for negotiated outcomes, not enforcement, and we appreciate the hair's breadth that can sit between the two. Nonetheless, others see us as soft.

But here, in this case, in my mind, there are still too many questions.

We board our respective Black Hawks and head for New York. However, Mike's will sweep off three-quarters of the way there to check out the crash site and confer with the National Transportation Safety Board.

During the flight, I call Alex to let him know what's occurred and for him to meet Jeff and me at our hotel, and then I phone Suzi to bring her up to speed. They all agree with me. Or, as Alex puts it, "It's well suss'." But it's late, and definitely time to move my body on from running on adrenaline. I feel nauseous and emotionally empty.

After being in flight for only five minutes, Mike phones my mobile. "Once we're done at the crash site, Dan and me will come find you at your hotel, and I'll spring for dinner."

"OK. But don't be far behind us," I say in a more conciliatory mood, "We're bloody starving."

SEVENTEEN

We land on top of FBI Plaza, as Alex calls it, go down to the road, and hail a yellow cab for the brief ride back to our hotel. It's just gone 3:00 a.m. and I'm relieved to be back in my room for a shower and change of clothes.

I've no sooner finished putting on my subtly badged FBI T-shirt gift from Mike when my mobile buzzes and his voice rings out. "Good evening, dear chap, fancy some supper?" Mike putting on his version of a British accent is all a bit Dick Van Dyke, but it still makes me smile.

"It's bloomin' three in the morning, Mike, where are we going to get dinner?"

"The city never sleeps, hungry?"

"I'm Hank Marvin. And maybe we can neck a couple of Jimmy Nails to quench my Geoff Hurst! Won't stay out too long; I'm cream crackered."

Mike bursts out laughing and returns to his New York drawl. "OK. I'm guessin' ya hungry. You can explain the limey lingo at dinner. Let's meet in the Plaza's restaurant—thirty minutes?"

"Splendid, old chap," I reply with a half-decent Oxbridge accent.

"Son of a bitch!" Mike shouts. "Text here from David at Bank of America. '*Urgent, call immediately.*' I'll call ya back."

While Mike's doing that, I text the dinner arrangements to Jeff and Alex, and then finish tarting myself up. Dark blue chinos and brown loafers so as to be comfortable, but still meet the restaurant's dress code: "No jeans, T-shirts, or sneakers. Slacks and black shoes required."

As I'm about to leave my room, my mobile rings. It's Mike, and he's already talking excitedly as I raise the phone to my ear. "Ya sitting down, buddy?"

"Don't tell me, the Bank of America are complaining we've not got their money back yet?"

"Nah, not exactly. They're getting reports from all over New York State that these damn twenty-dollar bills are turning up

94

everywhere!"

"What?"

"So far, six million. And at this rate, they figure they'll have it all back in three days!"

"Have they got the right bloody serial numbers?"

"Apparently. They've spent the last two hours auditing the data, and it all stacks up."

"Bloody hell! I just don't get it. What's the transaction size?"

"They're analysing that now, but first off, they had to check the data coming in from over a hundred and fifty branches. That alone gives forty grand a branch."

"This is so far from the archetypal blag; it really throws the cat among the pigeons. How the hell can this money be in circulation so quickly?"

"I dunno…maybe they're changing the bills? Twenties for fifties?"

"Could be, but surely this volume would raise questions in the bank's systems. Even at a thousand a time, it would take forty-eight thousand transactions to *launder* forty-eight million. It's just not slick enough for these slippery bastards."

"True."

With that, there's a knock on my door. "Hang on a tick, Mike." I let Alex and Jeff in and gesture that I'll just be one minute. They sit in the room's two red, paisley-pattern tub armchairs, and I continue. "Mike, that was Alex and Jeff. I'll bring them up to speed and see if we can come up with a brainwave before you arrive."

"OK. See you in half an hour."

**

Alex, Jeff, and I walk down to the hotel's Rose Club to have a pre-dinner drink—three tall and rocky Southern Comforts—comforting being the theme. I'm informed by the barkeep that this was once the Persian Room but has since been updated. Apparently, back in the day, it was a haunt of Duke Ellington and Miles Davis. The lighting is subdued, and there are cubicles with maroon crushed-velvet benches and chairs. The tables, and a lot of panelling, are dark rosewood, and it all sets the atmosphere of this tranquil cocoon. As I walk across the room to a quiet corner, I imagine the slow, gentle cadences of mellow jazz.

We sit chatting about the cash turning up, and we are all equally perplexed. Barely half an hour has passed when Mike turns up with a pasty-looking Dan, who informs us that Mike's obviously hungry—as during the ten-minute sprint from their office, they found the limits of adhesion of both the GMC's tyres and Dan's lunch to his stomach lining; at a couple of crossroads, they were both borderline!

Dan and Mike pick up drinks at the bar and order "the same again" for Alex, Jeff, and me. We have no sooner put the drinks on a tray when we are ushered to our pre-booked table in the Food Hall restaurant. I again crack my joke about being "Hank Marvin" and explain it is cockney rhyming slang: Hank Marvin—"starvin'." Then I have to explain the others I rolled out earlier.

A couple of minutes pass, and the waitress comes over to take our orders, which turn out to be mostly steaks. When she gets to me, she asks cheerily, "Hi, there. Steak for you?"

"Yes, please," I say eagerly. "I'll have the twelve-ounce Piedmontese rib-eye, thank you."

"Oh, what a lovely British accent," and, staring at me, "and how would you like your steak? Burnt to a crisp, or bloody as hell?"

That's one of my favourite lines from *Pulp Fiction*, and so I keep the joke going. "If a good vet can't bring it back to life—it's overcooked!"

That causes a chuckle all round, with the waitress declaring, "I'm gonna use that one!"

Within ten minutes, our meals are in front of us, and we tuck in like we've not eaten for weeks. The steak I'm gnawing on is huge, as is the bowl of hand-cut, twice-cooked chips. This meal is certainly satisfying my growling stomach.

Just about halfway through our main course, Mike's mobile rings. With a mouthful of steak and a look of frustration, he answers, "I'm having my goddamn dinner. *Be quick!* Oh, shit…oh, sorry…hi, Jackie…yes, no problem." After a second, and looking slightly awkward, he continues, "Hi, David, how are things?" Which is followed by the usual yep, nope, and so on.

After Mike finishes the call, he looks around the table and then takes us into his world of confusion. "As you'll have gathered, that was David, and this really is one for the books…basically, a lot of the money has come in via their cash-in-transit trucks during the past twenty-four hours—in one case, *during* the stand-off on Lewes Beach."

I clumsily clatter my knife and fork onto my plate. "*During* the stand-off! That can't be right!"

Dan raises a near-forgotten point. "What about the plane's crash site? Must be a shitload of money out there."

"I agree," Mike says, rubbing the back of his neck. "But before it could be confirmed, I had to let the NTSB (National Transportation Safety Board) go back to going through the wreckage; it's spread over three square miles, and a lot of it is still burning."

My gut's not happy, and it's not the cow I've just consumed. I lean forward and chip in, "My instinct says the bank's got something seriously wrong somewhere." We sit and chat around the subject while we finish our meal. But we're are all knackered, and it's not long before we decide to retire for the evening. We need fresh minds for tomorrow, when this is going to kick off big time.

Back in my room, I slump onto the bed and just lie there, staring up at the slow-flashing, almost hypnotic red lamp on the ceiling-mounted smoke detector.

I just hope I get some bloody sleep.

EIGHTEEN

Mike, Dan, and I are having breakfast in the Starbucks opposite the FBI headquarters on the corner of Federal Plaza and Worth Street. It's still bustling at 10:00 a.m., and we are lucky to get a window seat. We're no sooner perched on chrome bar stools with our wake-up espressos, than Mike's phone rings.

He has a brief conversation with the caller, and then, with a baffled look, turns to us. "That was the lead investigator for NTSB. He's completed the first run through the plane's black-box data. The autopilot was on when the plane hit the deck."

Dan frowns. "So? Almost every plane uses automatic controls. Pilots very rarely do take-off and landing themselves these days!"

"Yes." Mike pushes his plate to one side. "But apparently the auto take-off had been used, which is strange for a small airport like Monticello, and the auto landing was preset and initiated— again, such early activation is odd…" Dan and I are silent, brains churning, trying to come up with a feasible explanation. "So," Mike continues, "From the time the engines catapult the plane up the runway, right up to the time the F16 turns it into scrap metal, the whole autopiloting system is on…why?"

"OK," I say, taking the bait, "spill the beans."

Mike wipes his mouth on his serviette and throws it crumpled on his plate. "Well, after the investigator listened to the black box, he believes that the pilot *couldn't* turn off the autopilot system. And, the control system logging software shows over three hundred failed override attempts to manually throttle back the engines and change course."

With the last mouthfuls of breakfast now forgotten on my plate, I ask, "Why didn't the pilot just pull the circuit breakers? Even if that shut the engines down completely, at least he could then glide down and land—better than a missile up your arse."

Before Mike can answer, Dan unexpectedly leaps up and rushes out of the café. Through the window, we watch as he has an excited discussion with another agent. He returns beaming. "Guess what, guys? The G6 was stolen two months ago, and the gang hid the plane in one of the Monticello hangars."

Mike grins at him. "That's a long time in advance."

"Even stranger," Dan continues with a frown, "a second, almost identical G6 was stolen twenty-four hours later—not seen since."

Breakfast finished, we get takeaway coffees and stroll back to Mike's office to await our next update from the NTSB. Apparently, the investigator told Mike it will take a while, as the G6 wreckage needs to cool. But in fact, we've not long been in Mike's office when his mobile rings and the words *NTSB Inspector* pop up on its display. He puts the phone on his desk. "You're on speakerphone. So…tell me, how's it going at the crash site?"

"Not bad. But if this plane was carrying forty-eight mil in twenty-dollar bills, then it should look like a ton of very expensive confetti down here!"

"*Should?*"

"Exactly. No money—*anywhere.*"

"Shit!" Mike mutters, glancing at Dan and me. Then there's silence for a few seconds.

"There's more," the inspector continues. "We've found a large lump of switchgear—part of the circuit breaker panel for the plane's control systems—and it appears undamaged. However, on closer inspection, all the circuit breakers are stuck."

"That's obviously heat from the explosion distorting the plastic," Mike replies arrogantly.

"No. It's *undamaged.* It landed on soft pasture," the investigator says sharply. "The circuit breakers have all been superglued into their on position."

Dan and I are stunned at the gruesome implication, and Mike looks at me, aghast. "Shit, Lucas, your concerns are well founded. This is murder…" Then looking at his phone in the middle of the table, he asks, "Is that it?"

"That's not all," the investigator says smugly. "I've found out from air traffic control that there is a second G6."

"Yeah. We're aware of that," Mike says dismissively. "But, more importantly, where the frickin' hell is it?"

"I've found it," the investigator replies with relish.

Mike's jaw drops. "Son of a bitch…explain!"

The brief silence from the speakerphone suggests the investigator is savouring this fleeting moment of knowing more than the FBI. You can almost hear the smirk in his voice as he continues, "I was checking the flight plan, when I discovered the air traffic control log has two entries five minutes apart, both G6's, both from Monticello. The first flew northeast in practically the opposite direction to the second one you guys blew out of the sky only minutes later."

"Good job," Mike acknowledges reluctantly. "We'll take it from here." He closes the call and thumps his hand hard on the table. "Balls. Bet that first one is en route to the other side of the damn planet, and they've gained an eight-hour head start…shit, shit, shit!"

I share his feelings, and my instinct says the second G6 is going to the UK. "You're right, they are clever bastards, but so are we! I'll bring my team up to speed; let's see what they can come up with." Then, looking at them in turn, "In the meantime, you and Dan better get your bags packed to come to the UK." Then as I get up, I slap Mike on the shoulder. "Chance to practise your cockney, mate."

**

I leave Mike and Dan to their own devices and retreat again to the FBI canteen. I call Suzi and find that she and the team are already on this new lead. Apparently, she was emailed information from Coops regarding an intercepted message about the second G6.

Suzi continues apprehensively, "Look, going back to the heist itself. We all *believe* it took place at the SCC. Well, after hours of surfing the web, FBI databases, and CCTV, I finally got a break with the NBC TV crew footage. The results are *astonishing*."

"Astonishing?"

"Yes. I can *prove* they swapped the pallet at the back of the truck whilst the charade with the young girl was going on at the main gate."

"Wow! Pray tell."

"Where the NBC shot moves from the crowd to the main gates," she says excitedly, "it gives a glimpse of the young girl and the compound beyond. The action is very, very quick—in fact, I have less than thirty seconds of film."

"What action?"

"Well, there are two important elements in the shot. The first is a large, black line directly behind the truck, which I first assumed to be a power cable or something innocuous. But when you look closely and zoom in, there is a piece of red tape on a smaller, second wire running parallel with the first. With a bit of research, we found that this second cable is typical of the let-loose for a crane's hook release mechanism…" She gasps a breath. "When we measured the main cable, we found it's roughly the size for a sixty-ton crane, which would have a reach of thirty metres at three tons, and we're told the money weighs two and a half—"

"But five minutes, Suzi? Take a pallet out, unhook it, hook on another, and then crane that pallet back in without anyone noticing?"

"That was why we ruled it out initially. But…there's another view of *that* cable from a second TV camera a few minutes later. But here's the rub. This time, the control line has a blue tape marker."

"What?"

"It's a different crane!"

"Bloody hell Suzi…you've cracked it! Now, get that footage over to me straight away. I need to speak to Mike."

"Hang on, Lucas. There's still the mystery of how they get a kid to carry out that distraction whilst they do this ice-for-cash shuffle…"

"I know. Hang on. Don't tell, you've sussed that as well?"

"This bit was a pure fluke, but it does nail my theory. In one section of film, a cameraman catches the girl going past him into the crowd. He believes he's missed filming her, but in fact, he's corroborated this part of the heist."

"Come on Suzi, don't keep me dangling!"

"Very droll," she retorts. "Anyway, just as the cameraman loses interest and holds the camera down to his side, the crowd moves slightly. And, unknown to the cameraman, the little girl comes back into shot. She runs the last few steps up to a man, who bends down, and in big arms, he kisses her."

"What does that tell us? After all, he's consoling a distraught daughter—"

"He doesn't pick her up," she interrupts. "And he kisses her full on the lips!"

"OK, I grant you that's odd, but—"

"And…" she interrupts again, adamant. "If you zoom in, she's wearing a wedding band, and from her varnished nails and mature hands, she is actually a very petite married young woman masquerading in kids' clothes!"

"So…the husband could have helped get her into the compound."

"Absolutely," she says emphatically. "Anyway, the team already have a couple of satellite images taken an hour before the heist which show two cranes in an adjacent yard, along with a commercial chilled-food lorry in front of one of them— probably containing a pallet with two and a half tons of dry ice!"

"Suzi, you're a star, I owe you big-time!" I crow at her. "Will you send that footage and any notes you have to me straight away so I can show them to Mike?"

"I certainly will."

"Oh, and by the way—Jeff, Alex, Mike, and I are flying back tomorrow, as the heisters seem to be heading to the UK…if they aren't there already."

"Actually, Lucas, I have a theory about that too, but I need a little more time to verify some facts. I'll call you first thing tomorrow."

"No! Call me soon as you have something, no matter if it's half-baked."

"OK. Email's sent, speak tomorrow. I look forward to being

owed big-time!" I know she's only flirting, but it's good for my ego, and with a wry smile I gather my thoughts. I call Mike and explain Suzi's theory. He immediately sends out forensic and SWAT teams to the yard adjacent the SCC.

He also informs me that he has booked the FBI's G6 at JFK for us, which departs at noon today, arriving in London at midnight. Jokingly, he says we'll get to JFK by "Black Hawk Cab." He loves rubbing it in about the resources they have at the FBI and occasionally asks about British bobbies having wooden truncheons.

I must admit that I wish we had this seemingly bottomless pit of resources back home. However, I have peace of mind knowing that the best team in the world are working on this overnight back at MI5. And I expect they will keep the guys in GCHQ awake all night, as well.

My tiredness is overwhelming, and I look forward to catching up with some sleep on the plane. But there is still a niggling question in my mind: how many moves ahead have these bastards planned this caper?

NINETEEN

S itting in one of the GMCs in a private corner of the airport just before noon, Jeff, Alex, Mike, and I watch the FBI's sleek, black Gulfstream 650 taxi over. Its two tail-mounted Rolls-Royce engines are ready to thrust us on our way home to the UK. It stops in front of us, and the curved passenger door opens in a gentle arc down onto the tarmac as we drive the last hundred yards to its steps.

I enjoy the decadence of walking up the aluminium, non-slip treads of the world's fastest business jet, and I'm tempted to turn and wave at the agents below, but glancing over my shoulder and seeing their humourless faces, I refrain.

As I duck through the passenger door, the sheer opulence of the interior takes me by surprise. Sumptuous cream leather upholstery, plush carpet, and burr walnut-faced cupboards everywhere, utilising every nook and cranny. There are four rows of chairs, and then two sofas behind them facing each other across the gangway. The layout makes the space appear large, though in truth it's little wider than a super-king bed. At the rear is a door with a brass plaque engraved "Lounge," and a white-jacketed, armed "steward" sitting immediately outside.

We settle in our forward-facing seats, the door closes, we buckle up and take off. Mike and I find discussing this case frustrating, and so shortly after take-off, we decide to get some shut-eye. But it's not long before Mike's phone rings and startles us awake. He looks at the handset's screen, then at me, and mouths, "David." Getting up from his seat, he gestures for me to join him in the lounge.

The steward opens the door for us, and as we walk in, Mike places his unmuted phone on the oval table. This room is as sumptuous as the main cabin and has floor-to-ceiling LCD screens curved to follow the sides of the fuselage.

Without preamble, and in his usual businesslike manner, David informs us that his bank has now received nearly $38 million!

Mike breathes out a frustrated huff. "Hell…that's way higher than expected. Is the geographic spread the same?"

"No. That's growing too, and still no triggers for high amounts." David sighs, "It's incongruous. The resource required to make that number of separate deposits is enormous."

"Agreed," replies Mike. "You keep with tracing the money; we'll continue to track down the gang." Mike and I now sit silent, preoccupied. I can't get my head around the bills turning up at all, let alone in this volume. After a few minutes, Mike turns to me. "Hungry?"

"My stomach thinks my throat's been cut."

Smiling, he sticks his head out of the business lounge door and speaks to the steward. Fifteen minutes later, two huge steaks arrive, along with two slabs of New York cheesecake.

I've barely swallowed the last mouthful of cheesecake when my mobile rings; it's Tony at GCHQ. "Suzi tells me you've hitched a ride with the FBI—lucky sod!" he says enviously.

"Yeah, not an easy decision. First class, coddled in sumptuous cowhide and with fabulous food? Or cattle class, sitting on faux leather with a microwave breakfast roll…"

Tony gives a chuckle before saying impatiently, "Well, you better get here soon, 'cos I think a guy on your target G6—we nicknamed him 'Mr Numpty'—has dropped the ball."

"Why *Numpty*?"

"You're gonna love this. He turned his mobile on and then off almost immediately, but it gave a thirty-second transmission burst as the handset tried to log on to a network."

"OK, but what does that give us?"

"More like, what *doesn't* it give us?" Mike gestures to hear, so I put my mobile on the table as Tony continues. "Coops's hacked the mobile network, and that transmission gives us three masts and three sets of signal levels, which allows us to triangulate the position of the phone to within about one hundred metres. So we know the phone's over the south coast, travelling in a straight line, and at something near two hundred and fifty miles per hour."

"Brilliant," I say excitedly. "Get that info to Suzi, and let her know we're only a few hours away from Heathrow."

"Will do. Coops is also trawling for other nearby calls made at the same time."

"OK, and thank Coops for me. And tell her she's not phoned for a while."

Almost immediately, my mobile beeps and vibrates. I look down at its screen. A text reads, *Thanks Lucas, no problem. I'll call soon. Coops. xx.* She really is monitoring *everything*!

"Your guys are darned good," Mike admits reluctantly.

Fifteen minutes later, whilst tidying my papers into a folder, I hear my mobile ring again; this time it's the delightful Coops. "As you're flying into Heathrow, you could pop into Kemble. You know I live very near there, and you do owe me coffee. *At least* coffee!"

"Coops. You know there is nothing I would like more," I assure her, "but I've got this heist thing?"

"OK. But you realise this now escalates the situation to *dinner-red*—i.e., within one month!"

"That's a deal. I'm putting you on speakerphone…"

"I've checked for other calls in the same time frame as Numpty's, and I've found that a private mobile did an almost identical speed and direction only one minute later and is still on-air. The phone's been rapidly dropping speed down to a hundred and twenty miles an hour, and what's more, it's approaching Shoreham Airport in West Sussex."

"Nice one. But who's he calling?"

"Believe it or not, it's an Indian restaurant in Hove—the Ashoka on Church Street. He's ordered two curries, and his name is Wayne. Collection is in twenty minutes!"

"You're amazing, Coops." I say with admiration. "Better get that info to Suzi so she can get a team to meet him at Shoreham. Can you sort out comms for me so I can monitor everything on my iPad?" And again, in my best John Wayne impersonation: "*Well done, liddle lady.*" Mike grins and shakes his head at my American accent.

"Love it, Lucas," Coops replies with a smile in her voice. "I'll book us a restaurant, then?"

"Yeah, go for it—end of the month?"

Mike goes out into the cabin to make a call and bring his UK guys up to date. I stay in the lounge. Nothing to do now but wait for Suzi to confirm that her reception committee has picked up Wayne. I take this opportunity to check up on my girls back in Friston.

The home phone rings a few times; then Daisy answers. I can hear a mixture of pounding action music and machine-gun fire—another shoot-'em-up game, and no doubt she's trouncing some unsuspecting boy from school. "Hello," she says impatiently, no doubt juggling phone and game controller.

"Hi, how are you doing?"

"Oh, Dad…wait a second…" and the graphic sounds are muted. "Sorry about that, just playing a computer game."

"So I gathered. How are things there? You and Molly OK?"

"Yeah, we're fine."

"Are you OK for food?"

"Yeah, Mum's delivery came from Waitrose about an hour ago."

"No wine, I hope," I say with a nervous chuckle.

"Oh yes, got wine, but that's for when you and Mum get home." And sounding anxious, "Have you spoken to Mum? She's not answering her mobile and—"

"She's fine," I interrupt. "Her mobile battery has been playing up…I'll fix it when she gets back; I've a spare somewhere."

"OK. I will put a note on your desk. But…"

Following a short but uncomfortable silence, "What, Daisy?"

She gives a frustrated sigh, "I'm not stupid, you know, don't you think it's about time you two sorted things out!"

It's at moments like this that I wish they were teenage boys, who grunt, or at best give a simple a yes or no. "Don't worry, sweetheart. Mum just needs a little space…from me." I say in a reassuring tone, "She'll be back in a couple of days."

"Well, if she's not," she says with an air of mock defiance, "I'll invite my boyfriend round to share the wine!"

Like her mother, she knows precisely which buttons to press. "Don't try teasing me, I know you're too sensible to do anything silly. Look, I've got to go, so give my love to Molly."

"OK, Dad." Then begrudgingly, "Love you. Bye."

After a few minutes, Mike comes back into the lounge with a couple of lattes.

TWENTY

For the next thirty minutes, Mike and I discuss the ins and outs of this case. The gang seems to have considered every angle, almost knowing our next move. If we both didn't have *total* trust in our teams, we might think there is a leak.

I nip out of the lounge to the loo, and on my return, I stop in the cabin and sit next to Jeff to discuss the latest intel. Alex is fast asleep across the aisle. Jeff's online with his iPad, and after our deliberations—and aware of the gang's disregard for life—he emails kill orders to the MI5 agent that's going to meet Wayne and to our team going to Shoreham. Suzi and I are cc'd on that email, which arrives, making my phone beep.

I smile to myself, remembering that we offer targets a black, hooded fleece to get them out as inconspicuously as possible, and Alex always says, "They have a choice—body-warmer or body bag!" I leave Jeff with his other "cases" and return to Mike in the lounge.

I've no sooner sat down than my iPhone tap-dances across the table, and simultaneously, Coops's and Suzi's names come up on the display: a conference call. Suzi speaks first. "The MI5 and SAS teams are halfway to Shoreham airport. And I've got a local agent nearing the Ashoka, who I'll fully brief when we finish here."

Little does the gang know that our two crews are hammering towards them in two blacked-out Audi RS6s. "Excellent, Suzi." And looking down at my iPad on the table, "Coops…how about audiovisual for me?"

"You'll get two AV feeds, one from the MI5 team and their SAS pals, and one from our agent at the curry house. Each team leader has an AV lapel cam, so just tap on the multi-tile screen on your iPad to flip to the cam you want."

"Thank you, ladies. Speak later." And with that, I put my iPad on charge, prop it up on its integral stand, and sit back to watch the AV feed from the agent waiting outside the curry house. Casually, he approaches Wayne exiting the Ashoka and extends

109

his hand.

"Evening, Wayne. Don't make a noise," says the agent inches from his face, as he grips crushingly onto the handshake. "I'm MI5, and this is a Glock pressed to your ribcage. I'm authorised to kill rather than lose you."

"OK. Don't kill me. I'm married with a child…please, please, don't kill me." Releasing his vicelike grip and holstering the Glock, the agent turns and walks alongside Wayne, away from the restaurant.

The agent says softly, yet intimidatingly, "Be silent. I won't ask again. We're going to my car, so pretend to be a little drunk and comply *absolutely* with my instructions." Then, endeavouring to lighten the mood, "Let's go and have a nice chat." And gently sniffing, "Umm, Peshwari naan, my favourite."

In the car, the agent immediately radioes ahead to confirm his interview-room booking at the local police station in Holland Road, Hove. During the short drive, he outlines probable outcomes to Wayne—like extradition to the States, or maybe him disappearing completely.

At the police station, he drives down the ramp and then reverses into a bay in a dark corner of the rear car park, behind the main building. The station's night-duty sergeant, a portly, bearded man, beckons him and Wayne through the adjacent rear entrance. Once inside, he turns the car park lighting back on and then escorts them straight to their interview room. "Tea or coffee?" the sergeant asks when they're in the room.

"Coffee, please; milk and two sugars." The agent then turns to Wayne. "Same for you?"

Wayne nods nervously, scared to speak.

"Remember, Wayne, a constable's outside," and pointing to the CCTV cameras at the tops of two corners of the room, "and you're being monitored, so don't get cute." The agent then accompanies the sergeant to go get the drinks.

I click on a new tile that's just popped up on my iPad which is titled "IntRmAV" and then sit and watch Wayne stew. When the agent returns, Wayne looks more terrified. Who wouldn't?

The navy-blue walls, charcoal-grey ceiling, and black,

rubberised floor are oppressive, and the four basic stainless steel chairs look uncomfortable. The matching stainless steel table, with its central steel hoop for handcuffing suspects, is bolted to the floor. Even the small, bulletproof-glazed windows have matte black, vertical steel bars. Every effort is made to promote the occupant's feeling of isolation and vulnerability.

While they finish their drinks, the agent spends the time in seemingly idle chit-chat, but subtly reiterates the dire consequences should Wayne hamper his investigation. Wayne puts his empty cup on the table, and looking down at it, starts to open up. Apparently, he had been forced into this job after a minor gambling debt instigated by the gang got out of hand. Now he just wants his family safe and to get this whole thing behind him.

"So…" queries the agent, "what the hell happened with that first G6 in Monticello? What did you do that caused Homeland Security to shoot it down?"

"I only did what I was forced to do."

"I haven't got time for bullshit!" the agent barks as he leans forward. "What did you do, *exactly*?"

"OK, OK…I set the G6's navigation system to fly over New York and land at JFK and activated full autopilot, including take-off and landing. I then password-locked the plane's entire computer control system."

"All right, that's better. But how on earth did you get that G6 to take off right after yours, and just as the FBI SWAT team arrived?"

"Easy. I created a web interface to the G6 control system so that I could set the plane off via an app I wrote for my iPhone, basically making the G6 a drone!"

"And the timing—how so precise?"

"Again…easy. I also have an app that monitors keywords on the FBI frequencies. The Black Hawk pilot was kind enough to warn of his final approach to Monticello, so that's when we took off. We even heard that they were going to land from the south and put down in front of the hangars…"

Wayne suddenly appears to realise the gravity of what he's

111

admitting: *manslaughter*. He takes a couple of breaths before continuing. "Hearing the Black Hawk pilot tell SWAT to disembark, I set the G6 drone off."

"So…you've locked the controls, but why doesn't the pilot trip the circuit breakers?"

"I glued all the breakers into the on position. Nothing could be overridden."

"You seem to have thought of everything," says the agent, feeding Wayne's ego.

"Pretty much." Wayne allows himself a self-congratulatory micro-smile.

"When did they decide to let you off the plane?"

"We were about to cross southwest England, and still there was no news of our G6 on the FBI radio transmissions. That's when the boss proposed to drop me off at Shoreham Airport. He said that I'd kept to my end of the bargain and therefore he would allow me to go back to my wife and child."

"So your boss has a heart, after all?"

"I wouldn't go that far…"

The agent makes a couple more notes and then looks up and prompts, "Go on."

"As we were nearing Shoreham Airport, five miles from where my wife was at home in Hove, I decided to surprise her and order a curry. But I switched on the wrong mobile. I turned it off immediately and then made the call to the Ashoka on my own phone and—" Wayne stops in his tracks. "That's why I'm here now? You tracked me from that first mobile call?" Wayne's face shows that he comprehends the ramifications of that particular penny as it crashes into the ground. "Dead man walking," he mutters under his breath as he looks down at the table. And then looking up suddenly at the CCTV cameras, and then at the agent: "My family!" He drops his head into his hands and quietly sobs.

After a few minutes, Wayne manages to compose himself and declares with as much self-confidence as he can rally, "I need witness protection and new identities for me and my family." And nodding gently, "If you arrange that, I will explain how the proceeds are turning up all over New York State. No more until you get that sorted and signed by a judge."

The agent leans back in his seat and smiles. "I can do that, but I need to go speak with my boss. In the meantime, can I get you another coffee and something to eat? No cutlery, so you can't have your curry, but maybe a sandwich?"

"Not coffee, I can't stand the stuff. Tea, please, and a sandwich—*not* fish or salad."

Exiting the room, the agent gives the order to the constable, who returns a few minutes later with a very white free-vend tea and a prepacked sandwich labelled with yesterday's expiry date. It's difficult to say which looks the least inviting. Sometime later, the agent returns with a small folder. "Your tea and sandwich OK?"

"Yes. Thanks."

Glancing down the sheet that's paper-clipped to the front of the folder, the agent begins, "Right. Witness protection is agreed for you, your wife, and child. A formal document will be here within the hour after waking a local judge. While we wait for that, you will be taken down to a holding cell by the constable, who will remain outside your door."

Wayne nods and smiles with relief; then they leave the room for the holding cell.

I sit back in my seat for a minute and stretch my arms behind my head. We're taught to appear amicable and comply with our subject's wishes, but in this instance, I think one hour is a bit of a gamble.

**

I flick to the second of the multi-screens on my iPad and see our MI5 and SAS teams arrive at Shoreham. They can't see a G6 on the airfield, and at this time of night, they're finding it difficult to raise anyone by phone to advise their imminent arrival and to unlock the hangars. Obviously, they can *unlock* doors, but then they are difficult to lock again!

Eventually, the MI5 lead agent finds a sleepy-looking security guard in a small nightwatchman's hut. It's not much bigger than a portaloo and appears to be equally uncomfortable. He taps on its little Perspex window. "Good evening. We're looking for a G650?"

"Just wait a minute," the guard replies grouchily and without turning round. "I've only just come on shift, and I'll need to check the airport landing logs in the other office…but that's after I've put my bloody sarnies in the fridge."

"We're in a hurry."

"Aren't we just!" the guard replies sarcastically. "Keep your bloody hair on!"

"Look out of your little window to your left," says the agent menacingly, "*now!*" The guard turns to look at the agent, who pushes towards him a Met Police ID and eye-points towards the adjacent machine-gun toting SAS guy, who has momentarily moved forward out of the shadows.

"Oh, shit. Sorry, I didn't realise. Let's go to the office," and with a nervous smile, "I'm sure your colleague won't need a key."

Minutes later, the team is in a small room. It's like a Three Stooges sketch, with the guard falling over because the automatic lighting is slow to turn on, before they finally find the airport's logbook. Oddly, there's nothing about a G6, although there is a large refuel listed, but no time in the logbook. The MI5 agent checks in with his colleague interviewing Wayne and advises they are at Shoreham airport, but there's no sign of the G6.

While the significance of the missing plane percolates through my mind, Coops broadcasts a ticker-tape message across the bottom of my iPad's screen: *Tracking rogue G6 across France, originates from Sussex, possibly Shoreham.*

Mike nudges my elbow. "That must be them!"

"Agreed. But how the hell did they get in and out of Shoreham without a trace?"

The MI5 agent, seeing the same ticker tape on his phone, advises Suzi that the SAS team and his will return to London, except for his agent in Hove, who will continue to extract information from Wayne.

TWENTY ONE

Mike says something about stretching his legs and leaves the lounge for the cabin. I barely notice when he returns; I just nod when he says, "I've ordered a couple more lattes."

When our drinks arrive a few minutes later, I realise Mike's looking over my shoulder, staring at my iPad's screen. Just like me, he's engrossed in the holding-cell camera feed from the agent in Hove. This cell strikes us as similar to the interview room, but with an even more inhospitable air.

It's not long before the deadbolt on the door is unlocked, making a loud, metallic clank which reverberates around the hard walls of the room, causing Wayne to nearly jump out of his skin. The agent walks in and again adopts a caring attitude, hoping to make Wayne feel more at ease for the next stage of the interview. "Come on. Let's get you back to the interview room."

I flick to the agent's lapel cam as they go back up a staircase. Its bright blue, plastic handrail and pastel yellow walls remind me of my seventies secondary school. I switch back to the interview room's camera once they're inside.

They sit in the same chairs as earlier. There is a dossier and pen on the table in front of the agent, and in the middle a vended coffee and tea, a jug of water, and two glasses. The agent leans forward in his seat and pushes the official-looking manila folder a few inches towards Wayne, leaving one finger invitingly stroking the flap. "A cell is not the most comfortable of rooms. I hope you feel OK," the agent says quietly, still teasing at the file's tab. "We've been lucky…a very sleepy judge begrudgingly signed this document. Your wife, child, and you all get new identities and a relocation of your choice. But remember," he says in a less friendly tone, "if your information is false, this offer will be rescinded; you will be charged as a terrorist and extradited to the United States. That comes from *my* boss, and I can tell you from personal experience, it's no empty threat."

Mike and I share a look. We both know that's not *entirely* true;

extradition would be difficult and costly. But more worryingly for Wayne is that during that time, he would be on bail and sent home—easy pickings for the gang.

"Oh, I'm sure the document is fine, but perhaps just a glance?" says Wayne, spellbound by the agent's tab-tapping finger on the manila folder.

"Of course," says the agent. "But be quick. The clock is ticking."

Wayne scans the document and locates the small, pencilled crosses where he must sign with the biro from the table which he now rolls through his fingers like a nervous magician.

"Come on, time's up."

Wayne quickly signs the document. His shoulders drop, no doubt in relief for his wife and child's safety as much as his own.

"OK. Now spill the beans," demands the agent as he sits back in his seat.

Wayne swallows and shifts in his chair. "It all started a month ago in New York, with a software update."

"What update?"

"I needed to get my software onto the Brink's SCC system, and the easiest way is via a bogus software update."

"Ah, OK."

"I drop a professionally screen-printed update CD, addressed to the head of the IT department, into the trolley of an unsuspecting postie just before he enters the reception of the SCC building."

"How do you know they will load this unsolicited software update?"

"That's easy. The covering letter to the CD introduces an irresistible online competition: 'The first ten clients who install and register this update will be put into a prize-draw to win a special-edition iPad Air Retina 256 Gb and a Macbook Pro 15" Retina.' We also give the competition start date as the sixteenth November. However, he gets his package two days early, which means he believes he'll get the jump on everyone." Wayne smiles to himself briefly. "As it turns out, the guy entered his details on our website within an hour of the postie's delivery."

"What next?"

"We send him the iPad and Macbook, and he confirms receipt online via our installed app on the iPad. That program also informs him that if he leaves the app running on his iPad, it automatically enters him into the next six free weekly competitions. Sure enough, he wins on the second week—only a set of Bluetooth headphones—but that guarantees the app's kept running; he's totally unaware that I have full access to his network and main servers." Wayne sits back in his seat as if recalling the moment. "When the heist is over, I erase my software from their server, and after verifying I can't be traced, I totally fry the iPad's hard drive, making it a very expensive paperweight." He then pauses to sip some water, and, despite a wall sign to the contrary, asks for a cigarette.

The agent smiles and takes a packet of Marlboros and a lighter from his trouser pocket. He rolls a cigarette over the table to Wayne, takes one himself, and places his near-empty plastic coffee cup between them. "Use this," says the agent with a smile, and lights both their cigarettes as they lean across the table. "So…this your first break-bad?"

They both take a draw and seem to share the pleasure of a long-awaited smoke. Wayne relaxes back into his chair. "Before this terrifying escapade, I was a totally law-abiding citizen: not even a parking ticket. Then one day, I got carried away in an innocuous card game with a couple of new friends from the gym." He shrugs. "That's when it started…I couldn't repay them, and after several months of minor but illegal favours for them, they backed me into a corner."

He takes a long, slow drag, puffs the largest smoke ring I've seen, and then continues.

"They knew I had experience of SCC systems, and after offering several financial inducements—and me refusing—they made reference to my family; I had no choice but to comply."

The agent knows to be patient with Wayne's ramblings, as it's all part of the process of someone 'talking'. "It's not easy when your family's threatened," the agent says supportively. Then he takes a last drag before letting his finished cigarette fall with a plop and fizzle into the coffee dregs at the bottom of the plastic cup.

Wayne drops his fag butt in shortly afterwards. "I needed that. Thanks."

"I get most of what you said about this job," the agent continues, "but why's the money turning up everywhere?"

Wayne smirks. "It's simple, really. My software tracks the serial number database. On the day of the heist, it randomly takes one per cent of the previous week's twenty-dollar banknote numbers, up to a total value of forty-eight million, and substitutes them for those on the truck. After the heist, when Brink's and Bank of America do a trace on the serial numbers, they're already in circulation, miraculously turning up all over New York State."

"So the money that's turning up isn't in fact part of the heist!"

"Correct."

The agent turns away from Wayne and gives a brief wink to our camera. "OK, that's the end of the interview for now. A colleague has been assigned to you, along with a solicitor. They will manage the witness protection scheme." The agent takes Wayne to a far more comfortable cell with powder-blue walls and good lighting. There is a simple, hot meal waiting for him on the single bunk, and a steaming mug of tea and some biscuits on the adjacent shelf.

The agent stands in front of a mirror and advises me that he's signing off for now, and I turn off my iPad and end the audiovisual link to Hove.

Mike and I look at each another in disbelief, stunned at the apparent simplicity of this caper. I sit back in my seat. "You need to strong-arm Brink's to allow our team's access to their data for a forensic audit so that we can establish the *real* serial numbers."

"For sure," agrees Mike. My backstop plan is that if Brink's help is not forthcoming, then Suzi, or more likely, Coops, will have to get the data covertly.

Suzi's name pops up on my vibrating mobile. I answer and

ask her what she thought of the interview. "Brilliant," she says, "But, if possible, I need Mike to get that database of twenty-dollar-bill serial numbers."

Hearing his name and the words "if possible" in the same sentence, Mike's ears prick up. As he often says, "Everything is possible; it just requires resources." He gestures insistently to be part of the conversation.

"Suzi, I'll put you on speakerphone, as the man himself is here." And, putting my phone on the table, I nod for Mike to speak.

"Hi, Suzi, just wanna say your work has been…well…exceptional. There's always a job at the FBI if you get any hassle from Lucas."

"Thanks. But he's just a big, cuddly teddy bear!"

I chip in before she says something *I'll* regret. "OK, knock it off, appraisals aren't for three months!"

Suzi feigns a hurt sigh. "Anyway, Mike, please can you have a word with Brink's to release the database of twenty-dollar-bill serial numbers for the last fourteen days?"

"No problem. Give me ten minutes, and I'll get you guys some contact details."

"Thanks Mike…Lucas, I have a personal matter…"

I gesture *coffee* to Mike, and he peers out of the lounge door to catch the eye of the attendant, who happily obliges. I turn the speakerphone function off. "OK, Suzi. What's up?"

"I presume that if I don't hear back from Mike or you in ten minutes, I'm to get Coops on the case?"

"Abso-bloody-lutely. Speak later." Mike can probably guess but knows not to ask. The FBI would do the same.

Mike, on speakerphone, dials Robert at Brink's, who answers straight away. "Hi, Mike, what's up?"

"I require a *big* favour, and *quick*."

"Go for it."

"I need your serial number database of *all* twenty-dollar bills processed by the New York SCC in the last fourteen days."

"Hell, Mike, most things I can do, but that's millions of serial—"

119

"I'm not really *asking*," Mike interrupts. "The last thing I want is your next call coming from Homeland Security."

"OK, OK. Give me an email address and a cell number. I'll get one of my techs to get the data over to you. The encryption key will be phoned in separately."

Mike and I share a smile at the effect of the word *Homeland*. "Awesome. Thanks, Robert…remember Lucas from our meeting? He'll text you an email address and cell number for his colleague, Suzi." Still grinning, Mike calls Dan to let him know what's happening whilst I text Suzi's details to Robert.

Not much we can do now, and it's not long until we land in London. We go back into the main fuselage and strap ourselves into our seats. Jeff is just packing away his paperwork, but Alex is still asleep—how does he do that?

My mind, like a V8 firing on five cylinders, is trying, but struggling, to work out the gang's next steps.

TWENTY TWO

It's just gone midnight, and I'm still discussing the case with Mike as we jump into one of two dark blue, blacked-out Audi RS6s waiting outside a private FBI hangar at Heathrow airport. With discreet blues behind the radiator grille, we barrel over to Thames House in double-quick time.

Mike's guys are waiting in reception, and having relinquished their firearms after the usual protestations, they go with us up to the canteen for the team meet-and-greet. There's no queue at the café counter, and so we get coffees, push a couple of tables together, and pull up some chairs. After a lengthy discussion, both teams are convinced that the Italian Mafia is somehow behind this caper. But with time pressing, Mike's team and mine get takeaway drinks and go their separate ways.

I persuade Mike to have a proper cuppa instead of the crap tea they seem content with in the United States. And, after a few sips, he's impressed. We chat a while longer and finish our drinks before going to my team's office. I sit Mike at the private single pod immediately outside my door. MI5 and FBI collaborate, sometimes closely, but never share personal offices—not unless you want someone to accidentally see something you leave on your desk.

I phone Suzi and ask how she's getting on with tracing the cash. "Slow," she replies with frustration in her voice. "You would not *believe* how much goes in and out of that SCC."

"Well, I've got another little conundrum for you. Shoreham airport, and dropping off the techie so he can go see his wife and child."

"Disproportionate risk?" she replies astutely.

"Exactly! This is becoming like a Goldilocks effect: the clues have been *just* hard enough, the distances just long enough, and the timings just right."

"Agreed. I've said similar to Alex, and he reckons we are being played."

"But if it's not on the plane—then where?"

"Well, landing in darkness at that time of night would have given them good cover and a virtually empty airport. But they'd require either a large minibus or van, and they wouldn't want to travel too far; a tail light out and they're done for."

"Ah, good point Suzi. I'll call Alex and have a chat. He was in Brighton old bill for a few years." But before I can make the call, my phone beeps, and a *battery low* message pops up. As I lean forward to pick up my phone's charging plug, the energy-saving lighting switches off, causing me to fumble and drop the lead, which falls down behind the desk onto the floor.

I crawl under the desk, get the lead, thread it back up onto the top of the desk, and eventually plug the bloody phone in to charge. Finally, I have to wave my arms around to get the blasted lighting back on.

As I watch the fluorescent lamps flicker into life, it hits me.

The report from our guys at Shoreham airport mentioned automatic lighting.

I pull their paperwork up on my monitor.

Skimming back through statements, I'm reminded it was the security guard who tripped over because the automatic lights were a bit slow to come on. He went on to say that this had been caused by the lighting now being connected to the new security system. That's it! Check the data logs for the computerised lighting; I've found a trail.

I quickly call Suzi. Bugger. For the first time in two days, I have to leave a message about the possible trail on her voicemail. Then I dial Alex. "Weren't you in Brighton old bill for a few years?"

"Yeah, six, before the Met Police…" says Alex proudly. "And then MI5."

"If you were changing transport at Shoreham, what would you use? Where would you go?"

"Recently nicked white van—no one gives them a second look unless they're overly polite in traffic."

"Um…but where would you go?"

"Channel Tunnel's a possible, but that's a two-hour drive to Ashford and involves some heavy Border Agency checks; I doubt it's a risk they'd take willingly."

"True. So where?"

"Brighton Marina. That would be *my* first choice. Then a fast boat to France, giving you eight EC countries without border controls. Once there, then maybe a plain-Jane minibus—space for the cash and a couple of guys…and it would blend well across Europe."

"What more could you ask for?"

"Agreed. Nine hours to Italy, and half that to Switzerland—still my odds-on favourite!"

"I'll check the marina's boat-movement log. It's a tidal marina with only domestic traffic."

"Bloody hell, Alex," I shout excitedly. "That's it! Twice-daily tides, one thing they *can't* control. If the tide times line up, we've got 'em!" My gut is feeling better already.

"Just checked the tides on my iPhone, and it's eleven—perfect!"

"Brilliant, Alex. Get that intel to Suzi. I'll talk to the Central Directorate of Interior Intelligence (DCRI) in Paris and Interpol to get the ball rolling over there."

**

I've gone through the marina option with Mike, and he too feels that it's worthy of following up, but he's still more inclined to believe the money's still on the plane. I'm considering the impact of this investigation moving to France when Alex calls. "I'm in a cab. With you in fifteen minutes, but you need to know…hang on…tunnel…"

The call drops out. I wait impatiently.

"Sorry about that," Alex says, calling me back. "Suzi believes the G6 landed at Shoreham around nine and departed half an hour later. Based on a thirty-minute drive to Brighton Marina, they would have got there about ten, an hour before high tide."

"Next stop, France," I say, barely containing my eagerness.

"Yep. Dieppe is the shortest route, and less than two hours in a decent powerboat. So they'd arrive at about one in the morning and be en route through France at one thirty with four hours to Switzerland. But right now, only two hours ahead of us." And, with triumphant tone, "We can still do this, Lucas."

"Nice work, Alex."

"It was Coops who put the icing on the cake with data from the lighting control system at Shoreham airport and CCTV footage from a nearby factory showing a silhouette of a van next to a small plane. And finally, CCTV at the marina showing a boat being loaded!"

Brain whirring, I quickly scribble some notes into my iPad. "OK. First we're going to need flight clearance to Paris, so you get hold of your Interpol contacts and French Joint Air Command, and don't forget their restriction to four SAS men: the second four must be attired as Met police…I will clear us coming in hot with Bernard Moreau, the chief of DCRI."

I then go and track down Mike, who's wandered away from his private desk for a coffee, and find that Suzi has already briefed him. He offers whatever services we need from their offices in France, including F16s in their Spangdahlem airbase in Germany. It's obvious that he still has no qualms about blowing another G6 out of the sky. But using an F16 from a base in Germany to blow a domestic plane out of the sky over France is not the most politic option. After fifteen minutes, Mike, two FBI, and four SAS are in one Black Hawk. Alex, four Met-Police-uniformed SAS guys and me are strapped into the other.

Engines roar, rotor blades pummel the air, and we're pushed down into our seats as we take off. The rate of climb of these beasts is amazing whilst they simultaneously weave between office-tower blocks. I think the pilots should have T-shirts saying, "Fly it like ya stole it."

Within minutes, we've flown over the M25 and are thundering towards France across the Kent countryside. It's a clear moonlit night, and peering down, I see a never-ending patchwork quilt of pasture and ploughed fields, hedges, and copses interspersed with black, snaking roads and the occasional mirroring river. It truly is the garden of England.

I manage to switch my mind off briefly and enjoy the scenery until it disappears below the sea mist blowing in from the Dover Strait. Halfway across the English Channel, we hit some turbulence, and I'm aware of Alex sitting next to me, gripping his harness and groaning. I'm tempted to tease him about his fear of flying—or, as he insists it is, "fear of crashing."

Instead, I call Bernard at the DCRI. He informs me that several members of the public have seen a suspicious camper van. One phoned-in sighting concerns a camper leaving Dieppe two hours ago, and they got a partial registration number. DCRI now has all law enforcement agencies looking for this vehicle.

I tap Alex's shoulder, and he turns to look at me. "If they are aiming for Switzerland, we'll be at that border within minutes of the camper van, which leaves us precious wiggle room to recover the money whilst still on French soil."

Alex grimaces as we hit more turbulence, and the chopper bobs around like a food pellet in a fish pond, "Yeah…it's going…to be…close…need more…intel on the camper."

"First though, Orly Airbase, Paris, to meet with the chiefs of DCRI, CFA, and Interpol." I glance at my watch. "Our navigator says two hours, so ETA about half three this morning." After that, it's anyone's guess where we'll end up, but I've pre-booked refuelling at Dijon Airbase just in case we need to fly over the Swiss border.

Chatting to the navigator, I tell him I'm impressed with the crystal-clear intercoms, and he lets me try his helmet. The name of the helmet alone is great—*JedEyes*—and truly futuristic in that it has a retina-response head-up display. The pilot's helmet displays the terrain, flight, destination, and short-range targeting systems, whilst the navigator's can swap between complex navigational, long-range targeting systems, and incoming ordnance screens. The pilot additionally has the facility that his eye movement can target the chopper's side-cradle weaponry. This comprises a 7.62 mm minigun that can fire up to six thousand rounds a minute, and there's also a choice of air-to-air and air-to-ground missiles.

Both pilot and navigator helmet visors have the latest HUD (Head Up Display) terrain mapping, a bit like a car's satnav, but theirs also works when they look down through the airframe. They see an uninterrupted vista—seamless 360-by-360 views of the ground below. This also applies to the thermal imaging camera!

We have flown, with me dozing, for about one and a half hours when my mobile, connected to my helmet by Bluetooth, rings. "Good morning. I am Coops with today's in-flight entertainment."

"Hi…how is everything?" I reply, a little lacklustre. But I can hear in the background the indisputable sound of Coops playing with her Rubik's cube—no doubt the New York City map version generally regarded as the most difficult three by three by three.

"We are still monitoring the hell out of the airwaves. But at the moment, there's nothing specific." Then her tone changes from informative to sharp. "Lucas…have you slept?"

I swallow. "Yes…a little…what is there that's non-specific?"

"Suzi and I reckon the route the gang will take is from Dieppe to Berne, and from there on to Italy." I hear in the background the last twist of the now-completed cube, and a near-silent "Yes!" Then she continues, "We intercepted a snippet of a mobile message from Rome talking about a 'forty-eight-million-dollar crash-and-burn in Switzerland.'"

"Blimey. Poor sods. Plane or train?"

"I thought the same, initially, and skipped to the next interception. Suddenly, my voice analysis software finds a link to an earlier message. That message refers to 'forty-eight million burn Switzerland,' which still didn't make total sense, but it may somehow connect to our forty-eight million US dollars."

"So, what do you think's going on?"

"Think? Blooming well *know*, my fearless leader," she says cockily.

"Pray tell, liddle lady, I'm in suspenders here."

"I thought you reserved those for Friday nights in Brighton?"

"Not always Friday."

As usual, she makes me smile and raises my spirits. I glance at Alex, who has his eyebrows raised, and wink at him suggestively

126

as Coops continues. "Well, remember when you were lecturing in Cheltenham three hundred years ago and teaching me and other newbies? You emphasised listening: 'Above everything else, *listen*—don't just hear.'"

"Oh my God, yeah, that takes me back. But three hundred years…cheeky sod!"

"I remember one example vividly—namely, that of General George Armstrong Custer at the Battle of Little Bighorn. You said the reason General Terry's relief soldiers were late was a misheard message. Terry's signalmen thought the message read, 'Send three and four pence, we're going to a dance,' when in fact it was 'Send reinforcements, we're going to advance.' I know it's fictitious, but it made the point brilliantly!"

"Well, at least my message sank in!" I chuckle under my breath at memories of those early days. "But what are you implying?"

"Well, it's the same here. After listening to all the messages, it turns out it's 'forty-eight million cash into Berne,' which means the gang must be arranging a deposit in Berne, Switzerland."

She could be right. The team's wager had been on a bank in Berne, probably the Berner Kantonalbank—the fourth-largest bank in Switzerland. And they have an excellent reputation for discretion with numbered accounts. "That certainly sounds like our case." Then, tongue in cheek, "So…my years of tutorship did not fall on deaf ears, after all?"

"Yeah, yeah." Coops says defiantly, "The tutor wasn't bad. But he had one hell of a student, eh!"

"You're right there…anything else?"

"Blimey, you don't want much!"

"I've come to expect it from such a hell of a student!"

"Touché…" Coops giggles. "Well, my financial forensics show nothing of our money in the Swiss bank's systems. However, I did pull some CCTV from the BEKB in Berne which shows a camper van in the high-security underground car park. I had our lip-reader take a look at the footage, and she established that two customers at the bank manager's desk were discussing a deposit of some forty-eight-million dollars into a numbered bank account…the camper van left ten minutes ago."

"Bollocks. We're only thirty minutes—"

"There's something else," she interrupts. "The lip-reader picked up something as they turned to leave." There's the sound of her shuffling papers and tapping keystrokes. "It wasn't easy to decipher, as it was a wall mirror's reflection and the faces weren't always in shot, but she believes she got five words—*late, comatose, donating, good*, and *father*. Suzi and I think that one of the gang is hurt and has been left at a local priesthood. There certainly appeared to be two people in the camper van when it left the bank's car park."

"Where's the camper van now?"

"It's on their M6 heading south…could be Italy?"

"OK, Coops. This could be our big breakthrough—find that camper van!"

I sit back and mull over the new information and my understanding of Swiss law, which actually forbids bankers to disclose the existence of any accounts. If they do, prosecution is immediately initiated by the public attorney, who can mete out up to six months in prison with a fine of fifty thousand Swiss francs—thirty-five thousand pounds. However, since 2009 there's been an international agreement that any monies found to be proceeds of unlawful activity can be repatriated extremely quickly. Therefore, Bank of America, in liaison with the US government, will be able to lodge its claim—which should make it happy.

As for the camper van, its current direction suggests northern Italy. The roads there are certainly favoured by happy campers, so one more camper van won't be noticed. I arrange clearance for our investigation and presence on Swiss soil with the Swiss Guard and the Swiss Secret Service. (The latter's official title is actually the Information Service, but that doesn't fool anyone.)

By the time I've done this, I realise that we are approaching Dijon's NATO airbase, thank goodness, as the Black Hawks must be very close to their two-hundred-and-seventy-mile limit on their seven hundred gallons. This airfield is the oldest of the Armée de l'Air, having been established in 1914, and even before that, it operated as a civil airbase from 1910.

I glance at Alex, and whilst he's *looking* calm, he's still gripping his seat harness for dear life. But no one on the ground would guess he's so scared of flying, as after we land, he exits the chopper imitating the *Top Gun* slow-mo camera shot.

**

With the choppers and all of us refuelled, we reboard at just gone three thirty. Just as I buckle up, and with the rotors barely moving, my mobile rings. It's Coops. "More *good* news, I hope?" I say eagerly.

"Sort of…I think I've pieced it together correctly."

"Just say it as you see it."

"Well, it occurred to our guy doing the surveillance analysis that when following a truck, it's easy to spot it's loaded, as the tyres squab. That's why in his report he confirms the cash *was* dropped off, because when the camper van entered the bank, they did, but when it left, they didn't."

"OK," I say mockingly. "Keeping with you so far, Coops."

"Cheeky…anyway, something made him look back at the CCTV footage, and what he found is fascinating. The tyres did squab and indicated weight change; however, the ride height was unaltered. There was definitely *no* weight change."

"Oh, dear, that's bad news all round."

"Certainly rang alarm bells. So he dug further and discovered that the original weight calculation by the FBI and Brink's was based on hundred-dollar bills, but listening to the interview with Wayne, we know they're twenties."

"Blimey, that's gonna make a *huge* difference!"

"You bet. Whatever denomination, a bill's stats are one gram, and six by fifteen centimetres. Therefore, the lump of cash in twenty-dollar bills has a weight of twenty-four hundred kilograms—two point four tonnes—and a typical footprint of one square metre, half a metre high."

"That means a lorry," I say despondently. "So, does your guy have any explanations for the tyre squab?"

"He reckons they dropped the pressures, and then whilst in the bank's secure car park, pumped them up."

"Bollocks, bollocks, bollocks! I've already got the FBI and the US government chasing the Swiss government to repatriate the forty-eight mil."

"Sorry, wish we'd found this earlier."

"Don't worry," I assure her. "You guys have done great—it is what it is…but please, find me that bloody truck!"

Just before we take off, I advise the pilots that there's a change in destination; it's now Berne airport, and then I quickly update Mike and Alex on the call from Coops.

Now airborne, and hurtling towards the Swiss border, I sit restrained in my seat by the four-point harness, quietly fuming at having been hoodwinked yet *again*. And, to rub salt in the wound, I don't even know for certain right now if our new target is going to Berne or trundling off in a completely different direction.

TWENTY THREE

W e've arrive at Berne Air Force Base at 5:00 a.m., and while the Black Hawks are again being refuelled, Alex and I sit on the tarmac munching takeaways from the airport café while we wait for an update from Suzi or Coops on the truck's whereabouts. Mike's gone off to catch up with some of his local boys at a meeting room on the border of the airbase campus.

We still have an MI5 team shadowing the camper van, but increasingly, this seems a waste of resource. Finally, Coops rings, and I near choke on a lump of burger as I try to gulp it down. I cough, "Hi, Coops…" and spluttering, "Sorry…food down the wrong hole."

"Oh, OK," she says, surprised, and gives me a few seconds before continuing. "I've been doing some calculations, and crossing the channel from Brighton Marina to Dieppe and then from there to Berne doesn't stack up. Travelling by road, it takes nine hours to get from Dieppe to Berne. The camper van turned up in the Swiss bank's underground car park after only four and a half hours."

"So you're thinking these goons must have flown the money into a local airport in, or near, Switzerland?"

"Probably. But the only way to be certain is to go back and start where the trail breaks: Shoreham Airport and Brighton Marina."

"OK, Coops, I'll phone Suzi." I bring up Suzi's number and dial. "How's tricks?" I say, upbeat.

"Knackered," and huffing out a breath, "thank goodness for caffeine and chocolate."

"Oh…you *will* get on well with Coops!" I tell her I've been speaking to Coops, discussing how the gang got to Berne in four hours, and that I need a complete review of the intel, starting from Shoreham Airport.

"I had the same thought, Lucas, and we've just completed a re-examination. Unfortunately, *nothing* has flown out of Shoreham big enough to carry two and a half tonnes of cash."

131

I'm just beginning to think she's psychic, when there's a reverberating clang in my head as the penny drops. "Oh, bollocks. Except for their bloody G6 Gulfstream."

"Oh, sod it!" She exclaims. "Sorry, I must look like a spoon on a tray of scalpels."

"Me too, so don't worry. But now it leaves only two practical options. They dropped into a local airport and were met by a truck, or the cash is still on the G6. Whichever it is, we must find the truck and continue to track the plane."

"Agreed. The truck's lack of speed will give us a few hours' grace." Suzi sighs. "But there is a complication regarding the plane…"

"Go on…" I say glumly.

"I'm waiting for final confirmation from the FAA, but apparently, the plane changed *ownership* whilst over the Atlantic…"

"Shit. I sense there's more?"

"Too right! Basically, the plane is now owned by a Russian businessman who we know has high-ranking Russian mafia connections."

"Great," I say sarcastically. "The plane's heading for Russia, then?"

"Yes. Next stop, Dubai, and then, according to their lodged flight plan, to their final destination—Vladivostok." I need caffeine and let Suzi get on with chasing down the lorry.

I'm barely back from the canteen with a lukewarm triple espresso when my phone rings—this time it's Coops.

"Good news, fearless leader!" she says playfully. "We have just intercepted a call from a truck on the outskirts of Berne. The call connected to four-one, three-one, six-six-six, eleven, eleven, and the caller asked if the truck would fit under the maximum height restrictions to the car park entrance."

Despite copious amounts of caffeine, I am shattered. "It's been a long day, Coops. What number? What car park?"

"High-security underground car park in Berne; BEKB bank."

That gets my adrenaline flowing. "Bloody hell, Coops, the same bloody bank as that sodding camper! Get the local team on it straight away."

"Already have. Suzi says they'll be there in ten minutes, and she'll call you then."

"In that case, hopefully, we'll soon know if we have to force down a civilian jet or, preferably, merely impound a truck." My coffee's gone cold during the call, but I still gulp it down enthusiastically.

**

The next ten minutes felt more like thirty, waiting for Suzi to call me back. And I find myself repeating under my breath, "Please, please let *this* be the damn truck!"

When my mobile does finally ring, it isn't Suzi; it's Mike. "How's it going, buddy?" he asks.

"Not bad…we've got a bloody good lead on a truck at a Swiss bank. I'm waiting for confirmation that it's our target, so I can't talk right now!"

"Sure. I just want to let you know I've been liaising with Homeland. The F16s refuelled and trailing the G6, and they've authorised me to bring it down if necessary."

"Christ, Mike! A second plane? That would be an *unmitigated* disaster, and take some explaining to the powers that be!"

"Not necessarily," he assures me. "The G6 would be over the Arabian Sea and its disintegration attributed to a malfunction at fifty-one thousand feet. Our cover story would be supported because the G6 model has only recently been signed off on by the NTSB after engine failures in several other planes earlier this year."

"Well, I just hope we end this without creating another pile of scrap metal and dead bodies," I say vehemently.

"Yeah, sure," he replies coldly. "Let me know how it goes and if this truck's full of beans."

"Beans?"

"Twenty-dollar bills, buddy. You know, like what you call a *score*."

"I'm impressed. You've been brushing up on ya' cockney."

After speaking to Mike, I'm even more anxious for Suzi to ring. Finally, she does, but she's definitely not happy! "I've asked our team to shoot the bastard truck driver and passenger, for wasting my bloody time, but the team say it's not *righteous*."

"Whoa…calm down. Explain."

"Turns out the truck's totally bloody kosher."

"Oh!" I try unsuccessfully to hide my disappointment. "So they've tricked us again?"

"Yes!" she shouts. "They must be sodding wetting themselves laughing at us…and it's *what* they're delivering—a bloody industrial ice-making machine…and it's been paid for by a Russian oil company!" I sense her trying to control her rage. "And…" She draws a breath, and seething, continues her rant. "The *real* piss-take is, the machine weighs twenty-four hundred kilos, same as the cash. Can you believe the sheer fucking nerve of these bastards? Lucas, *please* let me shoot someone!"

"Steady. You're starting to sound like Mike."

I've never known her to get so wound up. I give her a moment as she catches her breath and her composure. I hear her take a deep breath. Then she says calmly, "Sorry for the outburst."

"No problem, it's getting to us all, especially knowing the swines played us *again*!"

"So…Lucas…what's our next move?"

"Mike's team will try and have a look in the G6 when it lands in Dubai. But if they can't, then when the plane gets to the Arabian Sea, it's game over for them."

"I know I lost it a bit there…" Suzi sighs heavily. "But I'm calm now. And something still feels wrong…we've missed something."

"Don't fret. Get some sleep, then get back on the case. You and the team are doing brilliantly—you will find the missing clue." Ending the call, I put my phone down and slump back into my seat.

I must have dozed for a few minutes when I'm startled by my phone ringing. It's Mike. "Buddy boy, how's it hanging?"

"The bloody truck's legit. Delivered a twenty-four-hundred-kilo ice-making machine, paid for by a Russian oil company…cheeky bastards!"

Mike can't resist a slight chuckle, then takes a slow breath and gives a gentle snort. "You know my orders. My boys will try and sneak a peek at the G6 in Dubai. But if they can't, then it's terminal engine failure."

This is so wrong. More dead bodies, and still no definitive answers. I try once more to prod Mike's conscience. "We *must* verify the money is on board. Otherwise, this will be the second G6 and crew vaporised in twenty-four hours."

"I have my orders. We need to clean this shit up, and quick!"

Exhausted and knowing I'll get nowhere with Mike on the subject, I go off to find the Berne Air Force Base café and one of its comfortable-looking sofas—I must sleep!

TWENTY FOUR

I wake with a start at the resounding clang of something metallic. Instantly awake, Glock in hand, my eyes search the room whilst I remain prostrate on a dark brown leather sofa. No one else here except a cleaner on the other side of the café picking up a swing-bin lid that she must have dropped on the floor. Luckily, she's busy gathering the spilt rubbish and doesn't notice me. I slide the Glock back into its holster.

This case, and the lack of sleep, is getting to me, and even the bloody sofa has given me a crick in the neck from my catnap.

It's now 6:00 a.m., and my first thoughts are of Helen. And stretching and looking up at the ceiling, I wish that she'd just turn her mobile back on so we could talk. But the agreement was that she has a complete break for a few days—no me, no kids, no school, no domestics.

After a few minutes, my focus, as it must be, is back on the case. Mike should land in Dubai in about two hours. But even that sits uncomfortably, as it's another G6, and I'm still waiting for his update on the cargo of the suspect plane.

The smell of cooked breakfast from the counter beckons, and starving, I succumb to an egg-and-bacon baguette, muffin, and my usual latte.

Back at my sofa, I consume the breakfast roll in a trice. My peculiar routine with the muffin takes a little longer. Off the muffin top, leaving two halves, and then cut those into quarters. I take a swig of coffee with each of the eight pieces of dissected muffin—something Helen teases me about. Again I have to drag my thoughts back to the case. Surely it can't be as simple as flying to Vladivostok and landing forty-eight million dollars richer.

My gut nudges me to review the data, and so I get out my iPad and start sketching. Egg-shaped circles for the main elements of the case, lines with arrows for connections, and small squares for dead ends—seem to be a lot of those. Then I redraw the lot in a rough timeline of events, countries, sailings, and flights.

I keep coming back to the plethora of transport. The identical-plane trick, then the van to the marina, then the camper van, then the lorry, and lastly, now again the bloody plane. Is all this really necessary to get to Vladivostok? That's what's been bugging me! Is Vladivostok really the destination? Given the origin was New York, why not fly due west to Vladivostok? They could make it there in half the time on the G6, and virtually no risk.

I summarise this in an email to Suzi and barely finish typing when she calls. Excited about my epiphany: "Just about to email you."

"Blimey, that Berne coffee's worked. Got those little grey cells a-bumping and a-grinding?"

"Very droll," I say sarcastically. "The destination being Vladivostok doesn't make sense. I'll send this email in a minute, and you tell me what *you* think. Anyway, why the call?"

"Just an update on the camper van."

"Is it still meandering around the Alps?"

"Pretty much. They're stopping occasionally for a comfort break and making reasonable time, but they're definitely not in any rush."

"That's no surprise, really. They've no doubt banked their ill-gotten fee long ago. Best we could do now is charge them with conspiracy. Even then a good brief would get them off, and maybe even secure some compensation for us 'harassing them on their holiday.' Anyway, here comes the email—let me know what you think."

Sometime later, I check my watch, and it's been forty minutes since my call and email to Suzi. So I grab another latte. I've just sat down when my mobile vibrates across the tabletop; it's Mike. "Hi there, limey. Shaking yet from all the joe? I bet you've been in a corner seat of that café for the last few hours."

"Yep…third cup. One more, and I'll do the 'wall of death' around the room."

"Now, that I'd like to see!"

"Did your guys sneak a peek in Dubai?"

"Nah, UAE officials are being sensitive about another plane in the same hangar. We could push it, but they'd get suspicious. If they found out about the money, they'd come up with some spurious reason to impound the plane and find the cash." I know what's coming next, and my stomach knots. "It's gonna have to be engine failure," he says dispassionately. "The Russians will freak, but they can only bare their teeth, since the money was stolen by a Russian mafia boss."

"*Alea iacta est.*"

"What? More cockney gobbledygook?"

"Latin: 'the die has been cast.'"

"Oh…right…anyhoo…the G6 is doing its preflight checks—take-off is in ten minutes. Pilot and two heavyset guys with the swagger of mafia."

"What of your F16?"

"Refuelled and back in a holding pattern at fifty-five thousand feet, with a second F16 on rotation."

I can't believe how detached he sounds. "So your guys sussed the actual flight path the G6 will take?"

"Hacked the pilot's iPad. Confirms they're heading over the Arabian Sea, where there's a tiny blind spot in the Russian radar system." And, like he's sharing tactics on a computer game, "I'll link you into my audiovisual feed so you can watch the action."

The AV stream immediately pops up on my iPad. Leaning forward over it as it's propped up on the coffee table, I stare at the "show" with horror. It strikes me that this is like watching a shoot-'em up game. It's no wonder soldiers, with this remote technology and drones, are becoming blasé about military campaigns. It's like paying with a credit card—the debt just doesn't seem real.

Mike gives me a running commentary as the G6 taxies out to the runway. No doubt Homeland has the same AV feed.

The plane brakes to near-stationary, then its engines roar, and it's off. It leaves terra firma and gains height rapidly, and it soon disappears through one of the dispersed, *Simpsons*-like fluffy clouds. At this point, I can just hear Mike on his direct radio link to the F16, agreeing on *very* specific coordinates: 20.382928 by

63.500977, before giving final clearance to destroy the G6.

He comes back to me on his mobile and says he needs a few moments with his team and that he will call me when the deed is done. The surveillance link drops and my screen goes blank, but I continue to stare at it.

In twenty minutes' time, the plane and its occupants will explode, and fragments of metal will fall to the sea like sparkly silver confetti. A few of these fragments will be red: human flesh. Despite being an atheist, I find myself quietly reciting the Lord's Prayer. And just about keeping my emotions in check.

I start counting the minutes. After eighteen, my mobile rings. "Job done," Mike announces coolly.

My whole world feels like it's been shattered by an asteroid. *Regnum Defende* is the motto of MI5—"defence of the realm." But this is cold-blooded murder and does not sit easy in my heart, making me silent for a few seconds.

"You there, buddy?" Mike asks cheerily.

"I'm OK!" I reply tersely, just about holding it together. "I'll pack up here and get my team back home. Guess you'll do the same."

"Yep. Just the paperwork now, and maybe some politics…you sure yer OK?"

"I'm fine."

"Just one thing," he says quietly. "And I won't be saying this to *anyone* back home. But my gut still isn't happy; dunno why."

"Mine too," I say, suppressing a maelstrom of rage and despair. "Speak later."

After sitting for a few minutes, I marshal my emotions and make a quick call to Alex, who is boarding the Black Hawk which will take him to join the team following the camper van. After that, the chopper will come back to join mine, and then we'll make our way back to Blighty.

Deep in thought, I take my time on the short walk to my digs.

**

Back in my hotel room, I'm just finishing repacking my overnight bag when I get a call from Suzi. "You're gonna love

139

this," she says ironically.

"Come on, spill."

"Your gut could be right; you need to get into that plane."

"Ah, now, that's a problem…"

"What? You're bloody MI5, surely no one can—"

"It's not that," I say, cutting her short, "the G6 suffered a FBI-induced engine failure at fifty-one thousand feet over the Arabian Sea."

"Bugger. We can't rule out the money was on it, but I don't think it was. There is one thing I do know: the serial numbers for the bills. It has taken a hell of a lot of hard work, but these serial numbers are *definitely* the right ones. Unfortunately, it blows the case wide open. We *must* inspect that camper van immediately—that's where the money is!"

"But we discounted the camper van…"

"I know, but we disregarded it based on the CCTV at the bank and Wayne's interview; we've not physically looked."

"Come on, Suzi, what's this all about? The camper van can't carry twenty-four hundred kilos."

"Exactly! But these serial numbers are for hundred-dollar bills. So we now have a weight of four hundred and eighty kilos. I'm abso-bloody-lutely a hundred per cent sure of that now."

"What, they somehow swapped twenty-dollar bills for hundreds? How the hell could they do that?"

"It's another illusion. Everything is fine with the SCC database, which shows hundred-dollar bills, including after the security truck is cleared over the weigh scales.

"Yeah, but we know that already."

"What I mean is that hundred-dollar bills are counted and loaded onto the pallet. That pallet is swapped with dry ice; then it's loaded onto the truck, and it drives over the weigh scales and then off down to Lewes Beach.

"OK. What am I missing?"

"Immediately *after* the weigh-scales confirmation, the data in the SCC system is modified to show that the money in the truck is twenties. According to the serial numbers, those bills were actually sent out five days earlier, hence why they start turning up in banks all over New York State. But the dry ice must have weighed the same as the original hundred-dollar bills: four hundred and eighty kilos."

"Shit. Now, that's a neat trick."

"Indeed. Everyone believes the computer! But, as Coops says, the computer is only as good as the programmer—who in this case is…Wayne!"

"So that's why they let him off at Shoreham…"

"Exactly. It was all part of the plan to get us to believe the heist was of twenty-dollar bills."

"And he's now got witness protection—which we can't bloody rescind…OK, get that camper van searched immediately. I don't care how or where, just don't let the FBI blow the bloody thing up!"

"My pleasure," she replies, elated. "I'll get hold of Alex."

With a wry grin and shaking my head in disbelief, I look out across the airfield and digest another inspired piece of misdirection. One wrong turn in my youth and I could have ended up the wrong side of the law, but I'm not sure I could construct a caper this complex.

The reality now is that we only have a small window of opportunity to catch these crooks and maybe recover the loot. I just hope our team still has that camper van in its sights.

Again my mobile chirps, and Alex beckons. "Hi, Lucas, good news and bad, take ya pick."

"Good, I need something bloody positive."

"Well, I am with a team in the first of our two cars, and we're only a few vehicles behind the camper van, approx one hundred metres."

"Cool. So the bad news?"

"It's one hundred metres of train carriage."

"What the bloody hell…"

"We're in a locked carriage. And in two minutes, we enter the Brig-Glis-Trasquera Simplon tunnel and lose comms—that is, until we come out the other side of the Alps into Italy, twenty kilometres away."

"Shit. OK. Prepare to search that camper van as soon as you

disembark; four hundred and eighty kilos of hundred-dollar bills should not be hard to spot."

"OK, Lucas. See you at—" and with that, the phone goes dead. Tunnel!

I immediately redial a missed call from Suzi, who answers straight away. "Lucas. I've been speaking to the Italian GIS, and they will have a team at Domodossola shortly before the train's arrival. Finally, we've got these bastards cornered."

"Indeed. We must *all* be on our A game now."

"I'll give you a call as soon as I hear from Alex. Though he'll probably phone you first, bellowing about crooks in handcuffs, swag in his boot, and a holler of 'More beer!'"

"I expect so…but if we pull this off, we'll all celebrate with dinner at Benares, in Berkeley Square. Get Tony and Coops up as well."

Anyway, I better round up the guys here and get the Black Hawks over to Domodossola.

TWENTY FIVE

The flight over the Alps is inspiring, and I find myself thinking how Helen and the girls would love this truly breathtaking scenery. Pure white snow layered on blue-grey rock with iridescent silver sparkles of meltwater as it cascades over waterfalls to the shimmering, crystal-blue lake below.

Suddenly, we hit severe turbulence which jolts me back to reality. I grab my harness while the chopper pilot struggles with his controls to maintain altitude, let alone stay on course. Finally, we clear the mountains and the ride settles, and I can now see the town of Domodossola, which is dominated by the rail terminal and its myriad of train lines and sidings.

The buildings are just like every other practical, prefab port in the world: concrete and tin with the odd splash of bold colour. The buildings' architects would say they were "minimalist," or where the paint is peeling, "shabby chic." Alex made me smile once when he said *minimalist* is just a posh word for "bugger-all" and *shabby chic* is posh for "old, tatty crap."

We swoop down and land in an empty car park, right next to a group of blacked-out vehicles—obviously Gruppo di Intervento Speciale. We all disembark, and I focus on locating the GIS team leader, who's hopefully forewarned the station's staff of the impending full inspection of carriage two's vehicles and occupants. The station manager won't be happy, but he won't argue with the GIS, who, like our SAS, will have arrived armed to the teeth.

As I near the GIS huddle, a guy turns to me, giving a non-committal smile, which I return. "I'm looking for Senior Field Agent Giustino Moreno."

Glancing down at his iPad, he swipes a couple of times, then replies, "Good morning, Mr Norton. I'm Luca." He turns slightly and gestures behind him. "You will find Mr Moreno in the GIS situation truck."

"Thank you. Can you tell me what vehicles are in the carriage with our camper van?"

He gives a small sigh and swipes his iPad once more. "With the camper van is a Fiat 500, a Lexus 450h, and a Toyota Prius."

"I presume you know that two of my teams are in their cars, nine carriages behind the camper van?"

"Indeed. They, too, are listed here on my manifest."

As I walk past him towards the gathered throng behind, I see Giustino standing next to the GIS truck, cigarette in hand. He's a typically fashionable Italian of medium height and build, with a mass of dark, wavy hair and a Mediterranean tan. With his distinctive Gucci 1943 leather-framed sunglasses, he's every bit the well-heeled, laid-back Italian. And as usual, he's wearing super-thin, made-to-measure body armour so as not to rumple his Armani suit.

Giustino—and virtually every other GIS person—has near-fluent English, though with an enchanting Italian lilt. Which, so legend has it, drives English women wild. Makes ya sick!

He spots me and immediately throws open his arms in a genuine, unfettered, and typically Italian welcome. "Magnifico! I was told you would be attending." He bellows emotionally, "It's been far too long, dear friend. Have you eaten? I'll get someone to grab you something from the café, their coffee is *eccellente*."

"I would love a coffee." Giustino shouts and gesticulates urgently to a colleague, who runs off towards the café. "It's been what—two years now, Giustino. How are you? And how's the family?"

"We are all very well, thank you. They would love to see you. Once we've dispensed with these *delinquenti*, you *must* come back to the house for dinner. I can get you flown back to London tomorrow."

"That's very tempting, but let's see how the next few hours go?"

"*Non c'è problema*. I gather these *suini* have been giving you the runaround?"

"Sure have, but now it's time to pay the piper!"

"Indeed," he says, glaring at the tunnel and gently nodding. Understanding the piper reference demonstrates his grasp of the English language. He then looks at me with a smile. "I trust life has been treating you and your *famiglia* well?"

"Fine; can't complain." And raising my hands contemptuously, "but if I did, who'd listen?"

"Very true, my friend…very true." And we laugh.

"I see you've deployed your squad, Giustino," I say as I look around. "I have two teams of SAS at your command should the need arise."

"That would be the norm: GIS as the lead agency. But when I found out it was my good friend Lucas who was coming here, I ordered command be transferred to you. All I ask is that you be gentle with my countrymen."

"Very kind, Giustino, but I will need to rely heavily on your advice, so I would prefer this to be a joint operation."

"Accepted. Let's get this done. Then I can take you home to reminisce on times past."

With that, we stroll over to the GIS command-and-control vehicle to review the AV streams being monitored by Giustino's team. There is a more relaxed pace with the GIS, but they seem well prepared, and so there is little to do now until the train arrives. Looking around, I count twenty GIS, five vehicles, and the command-and-control truck. Somewhat intimidating for the average tourist.

I phone Alex and leave a message advising the command structure and to get the SAS team leader to liaise with his opposite number. I emphasise that we are joint lead agency unless it goes pooh-faced, in which case all excrement will hit our fan. Usual politics, and nothing Giustino can influence.

He also tells me that there will be an announcement on the carriage speakers advising of a "fault" and that passengers and vehicles will disembark at both the front and rear of the train. This will allow time for both removal of unaffected passengers and Alex's team to get to the front of the train.

Ten minutes pass, and with Swiss-watch timing, the train exits the tunnel about a quarter mile distant. As it heads towards us, the GIS systems pick up the train's CCTV transmissions, which are immediately relayed to my own and the SAS iPads.

The carriages are unpainted, making the train glint saffron-yellow in the morning sun. And it writhes like a metallic snake as it slowly rounds the final banked curve to the terminal platform that is awash with black-body-armoured GIS and SAS.

Tapping on the first of the six CCTV camera images on my iPad, I see the platform-mounted "camera-1" is about twenty metres up line, front and driver's side of the train, giving me an unencumbered and crystal-clear HD view of virtually all carriages. The second platform-mounted "camera-2" has a similar view, but diagonally opposite, scrutinising the train's rear. Flipping to "camera-3," which is inside carriage two, I can see the front and driver's side of the camper van as we look rearward, with "camera-4" being diagonally opposite and showing the rear and passenger side. The picture quality is reasonable and occupants easily visible though not recognisable.

Except for the Fiat 500, which has only a driver, each of the remaining three vehicles have two occupants: seven in total.

Flicking quickly to "camera-5," I see the interior of the third-from-last carriage, some nine behind our suspects. Clearly visible are Alex and his two teams, all waving at the CCTV— a right load of pop stars. "camera-6" is diagonally opposite. My iPad shows mini versions of all six cameras, and with a double tap, any one of them becomes full screen.

The train arrives, and from the platform repeater speakers, I hear the on-train tannoy announce their arrival. "Good morning, and welcome to Domodossola. Unfortunately, due to a minor technical problem, passengers and vehicles must disembark from the rear of the train, except for carriages one and two, who will alight from the front. Thank you for your cooperation."

The train comes to a halt precisely on our platform's "mark," and we roll an eight-feet-high, twenty-feet-long screen between carriages two and three, thus shielding ourselves from public gaze.

Disembarkation of passengers and vehicles is mesmeric in its smooth efficiency. The rearward-departing vehicles form an orderly queue for the normal scrutiny, except with oversight by an armed GIS officer. The front carriages, however, get the full monty, including the unseen cross hairs of two GIS sniper teams

146

covering the scene from rooftops two hundred metres away.

Nothing is found to be out of place, and all vehicles, except carriage two's, slowly leave the station. There is a look of alarm on the faces of the passengers from the first carriage as they exit, which is only to be expected. But a general statement that "we are looking for asylum seekers" provokes the expected shrugging of shoulders and shaking of heads. The vehicles are given a thorough inspection along with their totally supportive occupants.

Fifteen minutes have passed, and we now only have carriage two to unload. Its vehicles are slowly brought out. The first one is a brand-new, pearlescent-white Toyota Prius. This contains two very pretty, mid-twenties, slim, tanned, bleached blondes with teeth that match the paintwork. When they get out of the car, which shows off their long, slender legs, eyebrows are raised. They lean back against the front wings of the car in their high heels, wearing *very* short white skirts and overfilled, low-cut, pastel pink sleeveless Ts.

Alex nudges me, and grinning, whispers, "Not a lot left to the imagination!" Instantly, the ladies captivate the GIS inspectors, who, *for some reason*, need to scrutinise every square millimetre of the vehicle in two teams. From the protracted and flirtatious discussions with the young women, it is evident that they are going to a photo shoot in Rome, and they are now running late. This immediately stimulates offers of a personal escort from *all* the GIS guys—these Italians! But despite turning the vehicle inside out, our teams have to let the ladies go.

Now the second vehicle emerges: a Fiat 500. Out roll two very large ladies in light summer dresses, wearing huge sunglasses. Again Alex nudges me and whispers, "Les Dawson and Dame Edna." A little unfair, but funny nonetheless. With two suitcases, carrier bags, and self-catering provisions on the back seat, I doubt there is spare room for a few parking meter coins. There are certainly fewer hands raised to carry out the body search than with the Prius! Nonetheless, we have to show due diligence, and the teams search every nook and cranny.

Now for the third car; after that, only the caravan.

This is going to take some searching: the Lexus 450h is a big motor. Driver and passenger look like an advert for Waitrose, with the chap driving sporting tan-punched-leather driving gloves, and the passenger with a scarf over her floppy, straw summer hat. This time I nudge Alex and whisper, "Bertie Wooster and Honoria Glossop." Whilst funny, this is just too twee for words—they are up to something.

The guy is a little haughty but nice enough. However, the woman takes the tack of "don't we know they're on holiday and haven't got time for this pathetic distraction." That is pretty much a red rag to a bull for the GIS guys, who take delight in damn near stripping the car—but nothing untoward is found.

I must admit I had to turn my head to stop laughing when I heard the scream from the plummy woman at the mere mention of a body search. She then seemed to go all Essex, with her shouting "Take your grubby little fucking hands off me, you fucking tart!" But in the end, it was completed with little fuss by said female officer.

I smile, remembering an incident just before my first daughter, Daisy, was born. I was in the maternity waiting room with Helen when a posh-sounding woman and a chap were taken to their delivery room. Some thirty minutes later, my wife and I travelled the same corridor, passing that same woman's room. However, this time she was on the "gas and air" and was shouting at her husband, "It's thanks to you I'm in this fucking way, and going through fucking agony!"

Back to reality and the camper van.

It's beckoned forward, but the vehicle does not move. The engine is off and the seated occupants unmoving. Our radios crackle as the SAS team leader whispers orders through his covert throat microphone, "Contain and breach. Form stick at the breach aspect." With that, he and three team members—the four-man stick—stand ready immediately outside the carriage's open doorway. The team leader has a shield and a Glock 21, the second guy a Benelli LS128A1 shotgun, and the third and fourth carry Heckler and Koch MP5 machine pistols.

They are all audio linked to an SAS operations officer twenty metres away who has a four-group of iPads giving him live CCTV views of carriage camera-3 and camera-4, as well as X-ray and thermal images of the vehicle and its occupants. He gives the team leader updates of target positions and their movements.

"Army!" shouts the team leader through the carriage door. "Exit the carriage with your hands above your heads. Do it now!"

"Ops. AV. No sound. No movement," advises the ops officer calmly.

The team leader whispers, "Nine-bangs. Now." He squats right at the doorway behind his shield, and with his right hand he throws the grenade into the carriage, which rolls down to the camper van. As he quickly pulls himself back behind the door frame, the deafening nine bangs reverberate through the carriage, along with nine blinding flashes that stream out through the carriage door.

"AV. No sound. No movement," advises the ops officer again. I recall from my training with the SAS that whenever a nine-bang goes off, people jump and sometimes scream. Something here is very, very wrong.

"X-ray and infrared," whispers the team leader.

"No heat signatures. No movement," replies the ops officer.

The team leader now refers to me for final authority to breach the carriage. I look over the ops officer's shoulder at his monitor. In these winter temperatures, you expect well-insulated bodies, but with hot faces and hands—varying shades of dark blue to red, cold to hot. In this case, however, the thermal camera shows only blue. Either there's no one in there, or they are dead.

With a mixture of nervousness and frustration, I give the order. "Breach. Repeat: breach!"

Immediately the team leader whispers, "Stand by…imminent movement." And with that, he and the other three team members don their breathing masks. He makes another underarm lob, throwing a CS canister into the carriage. With a rolling bounce, it hurtles noisily right down to the camper van and detonates with a dull boom, releasing plumes of eye-watering, choking orange nerve gas.

The team races in, checking the carriage is clear, and moves down to the camper van to wrench out the occupants. Moments later, they nonchalantly swagger out of the carriage and hurl driver and passenger face down onto the concrete platform.

Silence.

Everyone's standing stunned, looking down at the unmoving figures on the concrete.

Cardboard cut-outs!

"Perimeter teams, especially snipers!" Shouts a furious Giustino over the radio. "Sweep the border, shoot on sight. Preferably wound, but *no one* leaves this site."

But there are no sightings. The station's empty except for our teams.

I run over and speak to Giustino off-air. "This is impossible," I say indignantly. "How could they escape? We have the whole place surrounded!"

"They cannot get very far," he replies confidently. "At least you've got the camper and the *contanti*."

"Yes, thank goodness."

The radio crackles again. "SAS team leader. We've stripped the camper van, and except for a very large, empty Samsonite suitcase, there's nothing here. Repeat: no money."

I turn to Giustino with a heavy sigh. "Fuck! That makes it official. My day has totally gone down the shitter. Lost suspects. Lost cash. Bollocks."

Giustino looks at me and shrugs in disbelief. "Lucas, let's get coffee. Our guys can clear this *disordine*."

We walk in silence to the café, all the time my mind trying to work out where I've gone wrong.

How the hell am I going to explain this to London…

TWENTY SIX

G iustino and I have been in the café for about half an hour, pondering the events of the day, when Coops's name comes up on my buzzing mobile. "How are you, Coops? I guess you've heard the latest news?" I raise my eyebrows at Giustino.

"Well, I've heard that no one has actually seen the money yet," she replies, trying to remain positive. "So it could still be out there?"

"Possibly."

"You're OK, though, Lucas…aren't you?"

"Yeah, I'm hunky dory. Just tired and pissed off." Then, smiling at Giustino, "But my friend here is plying me with wine and his wife's fabulous pasta carbonara."

"Ah, that'll be Giustino. Well, get back home soon!" And with a mischievous tone, "And don't you forget that I've booked the restaurant for the end of the month!"

Giustino gives me a supportive slap on my shoulder. "Let's enjoy the rest of the evening. There's plenty of wine and a pudding to die for!"

"Oh, yes, I remember Bernadetta's puddings!"

Giustino raises his eyebrows and waves a mock-angry finger at me. Then we both chuckle. "In the morning, I will drop you at the airport, where my friend's pilot will fly you back to the UK." And with a grin, "It'll be quicker than a Black Hawk and more comfortable."

"If you're sure…that would be great." And with a nodding smile, "I owe you one…again!"

"What are friends for? And next time you're here, you can buy lunch."

**

We had a great evening, and just as important, I had a few hours' sleep. Then, after saying goodbye to Giustino and his family this morning, his driver took me to Ascona airport. It's

151

been a couple of hours now, and I'm nearing the Sussex coast in Giustino's friend's Gulfstream G450; at least it's not a G6.

I check my watch, as Helen should already be home; then suddenly my phone rings. It's her. "How are you?" I ask apprehensively.

"We need to talk," she replies brusquely. "Where are you?"

"Just flying into Shoreham. Landing in about ten minutes. Then home in forty-five."

"I could meet you at the Cuckmere Inn for lunch?"

"Perfect. See you there for twelve thirty?"

"OK. Bye."

Hell. That was short and sweet. But at last we've spoken, so maybe it'll be OK.

**

The landing at Shoreham airport is spot on time at eleven forty five, and as we taxi across to arrivals, I can see one of our cars waiting to pick me up. I wave my badge at customs, wander outside, and jump in our Audi RS6 which speeds me to Seaford and my rendezvous with Helen.

The Cuckmere Inn is allegedly a smugglers' inn and sits in an elevated position overlooking Cuckmere Haven and the river Cuckmere as it meanders in big, curling sweeps down to Seaford Head some two miles away. It's a semi-local venue, but I doubt it will have any patrons from our village. And if things go well, there is a romantic walk down to the Seven Sisters cliffs.

I meet Helen in the snug at twelve forty, and after a brief kiss on the cheek I refresh her glass of Pinot Grigio, get myself a pint of Harvey's Best, and grab a couple of menus. We decide not to eat after all, preferring to sit on a two-seat sofa next to the embers of the log fire. Helen snuggles under my arm.

Neither of us has slept much recently, and the stress of that and our day-to-day lives has made us both emotionally and physically exhausted. We sit and chat for nearly three hours, and through the occasional tear, she promises that she will do her best to be more understanding about my job. I promise to be

152

more open about my work and to try and be home more often.

We love each other, and we want to repair our marriage, but are we doing it for our daughters rather than ourselves? Who knows? But we are going to give it another try. Anyway, we need to get back to our girls; they are the important ones in all of this. They've been alone for several days, and in the knowledge of our marital problems.

Tomorrow I'm at the office to try and put this case to bed.

TWENTY SEVEN

Its 10:00 a.m., and nearly thirty-six hours since the debacle of capturing the "empty" camper van, but I've just put the phone down from Suzi, who believes she's finally cracked the case. She arrives at my office door for this final wash-up meeting. "Morning…all quiet on the western front?" And hands me a lukewarm coffee.

My mind wanders. "*Im Westen nichts Neues*," I quote the original German title of the book. Published after the First World War, it's about returning German soldiers and how detached they felt from civvy street. Not much changes.

Suzi enquires again, "Lucas…Lucas…you OK?"

"Sorry. Yes, I'm fine," I reply, startled back into reality. "I've swapped emails with Mike. He's already closed the case his end."

"So," shaking her head, "I presume he's sticking to the notion that the cash is still on the plane?"

"Yes…he says the insurers are compensating Bank of America, so everyone's happy."

"And we're expected to keep our heads down and go with the flow."

"Pretty much. So, from your earlier email, you still think the money was in the camper van? But if that's the case, then how the hell did they get it off the train?"

"I think I know. But if I'm wrong again, then this time I'll put my head back down below the parapet and agree with Mike."

"OK. Let's give it one more turn round the block."

"Checking back through Alex's interviews, it turns out that unwittingly, the train's senior and junior guards each let one of the two camper van men off the train." And with a vexed smile, "Before departure."

"That accounts for the disappearance of the two beardys. But what about the money? Did they somehow take it with them?"

"No hand luggage was taken by the beardys." Then she leans forward, smiling. "Either there was no money, or they left it on the train."

154

"OK. You've got me now. What else have you found?"

"A false beard, jacket, trousers, and cap tucked under a front seat of the camper van."

"What?"

"All the items are small, very small." Then—and her smile widens—"In fact, the trousers are women's size six! The forensics guys found blond hairs—female DNA—and very expensive fake tan on the flat cap."

"The beardys are women?"

"One theory is that a woman from the Prius, disguised as a beardy, drives the camper van onto the train. Then, during the guard's pre-departure walk around, he sees the beardy in the camper, then casually strolls down the rest of the carriage. When he arrives at the driver's door of the Prius, he's like a rabbit in headlights and doesn't see the passenger—having discarded the beard and cap—slide quietly into the passenger seat!"

"So the guard didn't notice *anything* out of the ordinary?"

"Well, in his statement, he did say the passenger seemed flustered, but she claimed being a little claustrophobic, and that's why she had the passenger door open."

"I must admit, it's plausible…"

"Yeah, the theory's good." Then, frowning, "Trouble is, the CCTV we've pulled from the train is through a lens covered in condensation and is just silhouette images of *people*. We can't determine any meaningful details—clothing, gender, build, or anything else."

We both sit back in our seats, sip our coffee, and in unison, go "*Yuck!*"

"Suzi, let's get a fresh brew and stretch our legs?" We wander off to the kitchenette, where I make a French press of coffee, and we chat generally about the weather, forthcoming weekends, and so on.

Then, out of the blue, and with a twinkle in her eye: "If I'm right *this* time, does that dinner for the team still apply?"

"Of course. Benares, I think, don't you?"

"Wow, that would be…"

At which point, one of the new juniors wanders in to get a

155

drink, and so we make our way back to my office. I sit and turn to Suzi. "Are there *any* useful images from the train's CCTV?"

"Not really. It's like looking through mist."

"Due to the cold of the tunnel?"

"Well, that's what we thought initially…but footage from other carriages is relatively fine."

"So why just carriage two?"

Again, Suzi shoots me that knowing grin. "After a total of two hours of reviewing CCTV from carriage two, we found the start of the action and see a person setting something up just below each of the cameras—maybe a flask." Then, looking at the steam coming off her coffee, "Within two minutes, the cold camera lens mists up."

"I'm surprised the train guards didn't notice this on their monitors."

"Apparently, it happens occasionally. The train was already in the tunnel, and it was only one carriage, so they didn't bother with it."

"So, during the time these cameras are misted up, the gang get the cash off the train?"

"Probably…but goodness knows how."

"There's something else we've just found out." Then, putting her coffee on my desk, "And this is a real kick in the teeth."

I lean back in my chair and let out a gentle sigh. "Go on, loose the worms from the tin."

"It's the hundred-dollar bills—well, their serial numbers—"

"Oh, Christ, don't tell me," I interrupt, exasperated. "Fake bloody serial numbers, what the—"

"No. Not fake," she interrupts. "Bank of America confirmed they are genuine."

"What, then?"

"They're from a week ago," she gulps, "and now turning up all over New York State."

"Same switch as the twenty-dollar bills!" Enraged, I look at the ceiling as if for divine guidance. "Clever fucking bastards! It'll be months before we establish the real serial numbers!"

After that bombshell, we chat generally for a while, and just as Suzi gets out of her seat to leave, my phone rings. I gesture for her to wait a minute. "Hello, Mr Norton…it's James."

"James?"

"I'm the guy who did your iMoCap a few days ago."

"Oh, yes…James…"

"How's things?"

"Not bad. I just called to apologise. I've screwed something up with it, and really need you to pop down so I can rerun it. Only take ten mins, tops."

"No problem." Then something strikes me, and I turn and look at the unmistakable black-and-white silhouette picture of Alfred Hitchcock on the bookcase behind me. Suzi sees me, looks at the same picture and then back at me, and frowns. "Actually, James, I've got a problem you may be able to shed some light on."

"Sure, Mr Norton, fire away."

"Can iMoCap track several people, not knowing who they are, but tell from dozens of unrelated images, if any are actually the same person?"

"Oh, yeah, easy-peasy," he says excitedly. "Just give me the footage and I will pair them off, or whatever."

"Thanks, James." I glance at Suzi, who nods, as she's made the same connection. "Suzi will email the CCTV to you…how long will it take?"

"I'll process it straight away, so, say thirty minutes. Depends how many people and how much footage."

I close the call and smile at Suzi. "OK, Lucas, I'll nip back to my office and get that footage to James."

I sit in silent anticipation until my phone startles me. It's James. "I've left a message on Suzi's phone but thought you'd want the results too."

"Excellent, what have you found?"

"All the footage inside carriage two belongs to five people, and the system's confidence index is ninety-six per cent, so it's pretty conclusive."

"OK. Thanks for looking at this so promptly, James."

There are so many questions, and my gut still says the money was in the camper van. And there are still more loose ends than in a disintegrating wig. I guess we'll just have to toe the line with Mike and presume the money was on the plane.

TWENTY EIGHT

It's now two months after Christmas, and three since the robbery, and here I am on the southern edge of Lake Como in Italy. I was invited to this celebrity fundraising party by my dear friend, Giustino. He believes it will be a distraction from the lingering memories of the heist, let alone my marriage problems, of which he's sympathetically aware. And to make it a boy's weekend, Giustino also very kindly invited Alex—and even arranged our accommodation at the nearby Villa d'Este.

The glitterati and their PR managers are strutting around, along with vetted reporters and photographers. And there is also the host's formidable yet unobtrusive private security, mostly ex-special forces, who will ensure the event goes off peacefully and that all audiovisual footage has final editing by the benefactor of this event: Johnny Depp.

There are dozens of A-list celebrities, along with agents, writers, producers, directors, and financiers. Some have been chauffeured only a few miles from their own Lake Como residences. This is certainly an event at which to be seen.

Despite work topics supposedly being banned, we've been chatting on and off during the evening about the events of two months ago, wondering if there was anything we missed. Giustino refuses to admit his GIS could have been hoodwinked, and therefore, *logically*, the money must be at the bottom of the Arabian Sea. Alex, though, like me, is more pragmatic, and convinced the money is somewhere in Italy.

Sitting on the patio and looking west to the lights of the main town, it's hard to believe the final scene of the heist played out less than half an hour's drive away.

Thinking of Helen and captivated by the sunset, I politely excuse myself and go for a palliative walk. The pale blue sky has a huge, egg-yolk sun slowly sliding behind the snow-capped, grey-green mountains. Its reflection on the water makes it appear to drip into the lake like zabaglione custard.

Listening to the water gently lapping at the lake's edge, I slip off and carry my shoes so that I can walk on the crystal-white sand, which feels like warm caster sugar. I start to become a little melancholy and decide to turn around and stroll back to the party.

As I near our host's home, I am struck by its lush, green gardens, with borders of pencil-thin Italian cypress trees and marble statues. The gravel paths around the lawns intersect at a magnificent fountain before they criss-cross up to the elegant terrazzo and across through the portico to the majestic, red-brick Tuscan mansion.

I finally arrive back at the private beach and see Giustino, who remained to chat with Alex. As I approach, Alex suggests we go and sit on the edge of the promenade, and so, like kids, we go and dangle our legs over the side of the lake wall. With only twenty feet of sand and pebbles to the water's edge, we goad each other to throw stones.

As Alex and I look around trying to find flat pebbles we can skim, Giustino glances back towards the mansion and says he can see two women that he may know. We all clamber back onto the promenade and stand and watch as they casually meander across the manicured lawn, somehow preventing their stilettos impaling the turf.

Alex and I also find they are in some way familiar and decide that we should talk to them, and that Giustino should take the lead. When the women get to within a few metres, Giustino, Alex, and I share an urgent glance. And I think: *the models from the Prius.*

"Good evening, ladies." Giustino welcomes them with a beguiling smile.

"Hi," the first of the two replies as she looks Alex and me up and down. And then back to Giustino, "Are you having a nice evening?"

"We are indeed having a great time…," replies Giustino, and gesturing to us, "This is Lucas and Alex. Work colleagues from the UK…" Then with a slight bow, "and I am Giustino from Milan."

"I am Allegra, and this is Caterina," she continues with a

slight raise of the chin. "What is your work?"

"We are security consultants," replies Giustino. She smirks, unimpressed.

Caterina, meanwhile, is more flirtatious, and does a "Diana" with a drop of the chin and a shy, doe-eyed, upward glance at Giustino. "Are you going over to the beach bar for cocktails?"

"Yes," replies Giustino with a smile. "May we escort you ladies?"

"Thank you. That would be nice," Caterina replies and grasps Giustino's arm.

We wander over to the bar at the water's edge, find an oval wicker table right next to the promenade, and arrange the chairs so that we all get a view of the lake. We sit and chat for some time, and while unremarkable company, it is obvious the ladies do not want for anything despite not having jobs or any tangible income. Maybe they just have wealthy and overprotective parents.

Whilst they have not recognised us, they are now preparing to call it a night, and Alex decides to politely unshackle his frustration. "So, how *did* the modelling assignment in Rome pan out? I presume it's now finished and you're both staying on for a holiday?"

Caterina frowns innocently at Alex. "What modelling assignment?"

Allegra, however, unfazed and with a hard stare, studies us in turn. But says nothing.

"Oh, I thought I saw you two on the alpine train a couple of months ago," Alex continues, "white Prius…you remember…it was the day with all those security guys?"

Allegra looks at Caterina and smirks. "Ah…yes, that modelling assignment."

"Do you still have that Prius?" Alex prods further, "You looked so Hollywood in that car." Caterina smiles at the thought of being seen as Hollywood.

Allegra grimaces at Alex. "Some stupid electrical problem…should have kept my Audi TT," she replies with the tone of a spoilt child. "Our father took it straight back to his garage when we got home."

"That's a shame," says Alex sarcastically. "A Prius is so fashionable." Allegra and Caterina ignore the comment, which now creates an awkward silence. Saying nothing, they slowly get up from their seats. "So," Alex quickly continues, "did you come here with your husbands?"

"We're not married," Caterina replies with an air of disappointment. "Our father—"

"This has been nice," snaps Allegra, now glaring at Alex, "but we must mingle. Have a safe journey home," she says with a hint of a veiled threat. "Ciao, ciao." Despite her bravado, Allegra looks nervously at Caterina as they turn to walk away.

Alex nudges Giustino, and pulling out his iPhone, whispers "Video."

Seeing Alex pointing his iPhone at the women, Giustino instinctively shouts, "Ladies, I hate to see you go, but I love to watch you leave!"

Allegra and Caterina shoot an over-the-shoulder, contemptuous smile, then turn sharp left to stride across the verdant lawns and continue back towards the mansion. "That may just be enough footage," says Alex as he emails a copy of the video back to Suzi to get it analysed.

After running back to reception, Giustino's badge clears our way to check the guest list, and sure enough, the two women are listed—Caterina and Allegra Bianchi, from a major Mafia family. And they've already left for the evening.

There's nothing else we can do now but wait for a reply from Suzi, and so we stay and enjoy the fifty grand's worth of fireworks that close the end of this fantastic party.

**

It's only been twenty minutes, and my mobile shakes my jacket pocket: it's Suzi. "What have you found?" I bark before she has time to speak.

"They are definitely the two women from carriage two, confirmed by James and the iMoCap. Also, putting the images through facial recognition, they come up as the daughters of Como Mafia family Bianchi—" I hear a door slam in the background making her gasp. "What the—!" she shouts, before calmly adding, "Oh, it's you, James. Hang on a second, Lucas…" I can hear a very brief, muffled discussion in the background, and then she continues, "James wants a word with you, Lucas…I'll put us on speakerphone."

"Mr Norton," says a breathless James, "just after I ran these girls through the iMoCap system, it went off and found a secondary relationship to my earlier analysis. I've checked this three times, and it's staggering."

"Staggering?" I ask, surprised.

"Bloomin' right, Mr Norton. It's calculated a ninety-eight per cent correlation on those two women making some ten journeys from the camper to the Prius."

Suddenly, two things dawn on me: *empty* suitcase and *electrical* problem! "Bloody hell," I shout, "we've found the missing pieces of the jigsaw!"

I turn and look at Alex, who mouths, "Battery." Two minds with a single thought.

"I bet the Prius lithium battery compartment was just an empty, carbon-fibre casing, which the women filled with the cash. Ten trips with the suitcase!" And sarcastically, but with a smile, "And we bloody well waved them on their way!" Overexcited at finally solving the case, we eventually say our farewells and close the call.

After chatting for a while and polishing off a few celebratory drinks, Giustino arranges a cab for Alex and me back to our hotel.

I suspect the car, like the money, is long gone, both laundered—the former in a crusher. But what a day.

Now I will sleep!

The End

AUTHOR BIOGRAPHY

Martin Link earned a BA in Technology from the Open University in support of his nineteen-year career with the Post Office. He studied analogue and digital electronics, as well as materials science.

He has been involved in security matters at very high levels, including building security, cash centers, and with large blue-chip companies. He has always been fascinated with the premise of something being "impenetrable".

Link brings this expertise in security to bear in his debut novel. Misdirection is the first in a series of international crime thrillers that follow MI5 agent Lucas Norton as he chases down high-tech criminals while dealing with life's everyday problems at home. Link sees his protagonist as a modern-day Bond, except that he is someone with whom the reader can identify as a regular person.

 Martinlinkbooks   @linkbooks    www.martinlink.co.uk

Printed in Great Britain
by Amazon